Vanderpull and the Baked Escape

Martin Stewart
illustrated by David Habben

Penguin Workshop

PENGUIN WORKSHOP
An imprint of Penguin Random House LLC
1745 Broadway, New York, New York 10019

First published in the United Kingdom by Zephyr,
an imprint of Head of Zeus Ltd, part of Bloomsbury Plc, 2023

First published in the United States of America by Penguin Workshop,
an imprint of Penguin Random House LLC, 2025

Text copyright © 2023 by Martin Stewart
Illustrations copyright © 2023 by David Habben

Penguin Random House values and supports copyright. Copyright fuels creativity, encourages diverse voices, promotes free speech, and creates a vibrant culture. Thank you for buying an authorized edition of this book and for complying with copyright laws by not reproducing, scanning, or distributing any part of it in any form without permission. You are supporting writers and allowing Penguin Random House to continue to publish books for every reader. Please note that no part of this book may be used or reproduced in any manner for the purpose of training artificial intelligence technologies or systems.

PENGUIN is a registered trademark and PENGUIN WORKSHOP is a trademark of Penguin Books Ltd, and the W colophon is a registered trademark of Penguin Random House LLC.

Visit us online at penguinrandomhouse.com.

Library of Congress Cataloging-in-Publication Data is available.

Printed in the United States of America

ISBN 9780593754085

1st Printing

LSCC

This book is a work of fiction. Any references to historical events, real people, or real places are used fictitiously. Other names, characters, places, and events are products of the author's imagination, and any resemblance to actual events or places or persons, living or dead, is entirely coincidental.

The publisher does not have any control over and does not assume any responsibility for author or third-party websites or their content.

For Tessie

PART ONE

Miss Acrid's Orphanage for Errant Childs

1

A Daring Rescue

bear traps ✱ lockpicks ✱ stuffed dodos

The world outside was swollen with new snow, and its light cut the room like a torch beam. Bridget Baxter slid a lockpick from her teeth.

"How much longer?" whispered Tom.

"Just a couple of minutes."

"You said that a couple of minutes ago."

Bridget raised an eyebrow. Tom clamped his hands over his mouth.

"I'm going as fast as I can, and besides," Bridget checked the Listening Glass[1] she'd slipped under

---

[1] A long, stethoscope-like object of Bridget's own invention, the Listening Glass enabled the user to listen round corners, eavesdrop on secrets and keep a lookout during acts of mischief.

the door, "she's not even in the corridor yet. Calm down."

"*Calm down?*" hissed Tom. "You're not the one with your leg in a bear trap! And for *what?* Talking with my mouth full of breakfast?"

"*Singing* with your mouth full," corrected Bridget. She reached into her thicket of orange hair, found a tweezle-tip lockpick, and eased it into the enormous padlock. "And you *were* standing on the table."

Tom shrugged.

"I had to make sure everyone could hear me."

They giggled silently. Dust sank through the snow-light and settled on Miss Acrid's many hideous things.

On the badly stuffed birds and unread books.

On the stern marble busts and murky paintings.

On the jars of eyeballs and cat-skull cups.

And on Miss Acrid's gigantic, soggy sandwich.[2] Bridget looked at the sandwich, which sat in the center of Miss Acrid's enormous desk.

---

[2] Miss Acrid's *only* food was tinned-fish sandwiches — herring and egg muffin for breakfast, anchovy and gherkin panini for lunch, mackerel and cabbage cobbler for dinner — and consequently she continuously carried a suffocating seafood stink.

Shuddering, she closed her eyes and let her mind drift into her lockpicking hand, shutting down her senses until all that remained was the skin of her fingertips—five little antennas, listening to the lock's secret whispers.

"What are you *doing*?" whispered Tom urgently.

"You don't use your eyes to see inside a lock," said Bridget softly. "You see through your fingers."

"You read that somewhere, didn't you?"

"Of course."

"In a big, long book?"

"Yes," said Bridget. "A wonderful book, full of bravery and love and fun."

"And padlocks?"

"Yes. Now shush—I'm trying to listen."

"Through your fingers?"

"Yes!" hissed Bridget. "Are you *incapable* of silence?"

Tom picked the feathers from a stuffed dodo.

"The Families are coming today," he said. "Last time, Poppy Parker went to live on Easy Street."

"That's not a real street, you know," said Bridget. "It just means her new parents are rich."

Bridget remembered it well: Poppy had been whisked away in a handsome, electric airship. Bridget had watched from her hiding spot among the library's chimneys and gargoyles, following the airship's gleaming copper past the village of Belle-on-Sea, toward the great towns and cities beyond the hills.

She thought about the people who came to the Orphanage only once a year, looking for children to love. She imagined their caramel coats and comfortable houses; their glossy hair and wide smiles; how she wished a sweet-smelling family would spread their arms, wrap her in the tightest most wonderful hug—and take her far, far away from the Orphanage for Errant Childs.[3]

But she shook her head, scattering the vision. A shower of sparks burped from the fire.

"What are you thinking about?" said Tom.

Bridget paused for a moment. Tom squeezed her shoulder.

"Maybe this time—"

"This time will be the same as all the others," said Bridget, turning her attention back to the lock. "Whenever the Families come, Miss Acrid makes sure I'm shut away, or helping the janitor, or . . . climbing the chimney stacks! It's never my turn. I'll never find a real home. I've already been here *nine* years."

"But that isn't so long, really, I mean, some people live to a hundred. Some tortoises live to two hundred! And some rocks have been around since—"

"I'm not a tortoise, though," said Bridget, twisting

---

[3] Miss Acrid stubbornly refused to change the Orphanage's name to the "Orphanage for Errant *Children*." She had a powerful hatred of irregular plurals, and whenever persons corrected her (like the time she complained to Mrs. Pobydd about an infestation of mouses), she would angrily gnash her tooths.

the lockpick with a *sproink*, "or a pebble. When you're nine years old, nine years is forever—I've been here *forever*. And forever is for ever and that's that. I've seen *countless* Childs find new families, and I— What are you *doing* to that dodo?"

"I'm trying to make him look like Miss Acrid," said Tom, wrinkling his nose and leaning away from the stuffed bird. Its eyes had narrowed, and the eyebrows were closer together.

"That's pretty good," said Bridget. "It's just right. Sort of . . . surprised about being constipated."

Tom pushed the dodo's eyebrows even closer and puffed out its cheeks.

"You always get the better of Miss Acrid.[4] How many times have you been thrown into the dungeon?"

Bridget shrugged.

---

[4] Where other institutions might have a Roll of Honor, the Orphanage for Errant Childs had *Miss Acrid's Roll of Horrid Enemies*, upon which the name of that year's most defiant occupant was scrawled in big black letters. The *Roll of Horrid Enemies* was nine years old, so it was little more than a board on which Mr. Falstaff, the janitor, had written "Bridget Baxter" nine times.

"I stopped counting after the first hundred."

"Remember when she dropped you in the Bottomless Pit? You were back in her office before she was!"

"Well," said Bridget modestly, "she shouldn't call it *bottomless* if—"

"I can't *believe* you hid her Mistress medallion!"

"You'd think," said Bridget, "she would *check* her sandwiches—"

"And what did she say when you filled all her teabags with glitter?"

Bridget hopped to her feet, pulling her unruly hair over her ears.

"*Baxter!*" she cried, in perfect imitation of Miss Acrid's shrill and shrieky voice. "*Whaaaaii is my break-fast-brew so spark-elly and shyyy-naaaaaay?*"

They giggled again.

"You will find a real home, Bridget," said Tom. "I know you will."

Bridget's tummy knotted up tight, and she blinked very quickly.

"We both will," she managed. "We'll—"

She turned her head.

"What?" said Tom. "What is it?"

Bridget grabbed the Listening Glass: footsteps—unmistakably Miss Acrid's—thundered in her ears.

"She's coming!"

"Oh, *no*!" whispered Tom. "Run, Bridget—go! There's no sense in you getting caught when it was me who—"

But Bridget was already kneeling beside the bear trap, eyes tightly shut.

"Bridget—"

"Ssh!"

The Listening Glass was hopping on the floor.

"Go! You needn't—"

"*Sssshh!*" hissed Bridget.

Trying to ignore the rumble of approaching boots, she followed the clever little pattern of the padlock's pins, working the lockpick with twists and tickles and taps until, with a satisfying, solid *thunk*, the pins sang their secret song—and the padlock fell apart.

"You did it!" cried Tom, rubbing his leg as Miss

Acrid's footsteps drew nearer. "But *now* what do we do? We're trapped!"

Bridget kicked the window, which swung open with a scrape of powdery snow.

A sharp wind cut the children's cheeks.

"Out of the *window*?" said Tom. "But—"

"I made this from a thousand elastic bands," said Bridget, unwinding a long rope from around her waist, "for exactly this situation."

"You made this so we could jump out of Miss Acrid's window after you'd freed me from a bear trap I got put in for singing 'Look Out, Mr. Chipmunk!' while standing on a three-legged table with one foot in a bowl of cold porridge and the other on a piece of burnt toast?"

"Well, maybe not *exactly* this situation," said Bridget, tying one end of the rope to Miss Acrid's enormous desk, and the other around Tom's middle.

Tom peered uncertainly into the gardens. The distant trees looked like pieces of frosted broccoli, and the Great Maze—a wintery labyrinth of thickets and leaves—sprawled toward the horizon.

"Will it take my weight?" he said.

"Definitely," said Bridget. Then, because she

never lied, added, "Probably."

"*Probably?*" screamed Tom, vanishing out the window.

The door burst open.

Miss Acrid, her battleship bosom trembling with rage, her battle-ax nose flaring and high, burst into the room.

"*Baxter?*" she screamed, flexing her grubby fists. "*This* time you've gone *too far*! I'm—"

Bridget picked up the Mistress's disgusting breakfast sandwich. It was heavy and wet and smelled like rotting seaweed.

Miss Acrid froze.

"Now, Baxter . . ." she said carefully, "don't do anything silly."

"Silly like what?" said Bridget. "Silly like eat your horrible breakfast?"

Miss Acrid took a clomp forward.

"You don't want to do something you'll regret," she said.

She took another clomp, her giant boot throwing up a cloud of dust.

"Is that so?" said Bridget.

Miss Acrid's eyes widened.

"Be *sensible*," she snarled. "And . . . put . . . down . . . my . . . breakfast."

Bridget stared into the Mistress's black eyes.

"You know, Miss Acrid," she said. "I read somewhere that you only regret the things you *don't* do."

And she bit so far into the disgusting sandwich the crusts touched her ears.

Miss Acrid went purple, mouth flapping as she filled her lungs with one of her legendary screams.

Bridget hopped onto the enormous desk—and jumped out the window.

2

The Kwassong

paraskirt ✳ the Great Maze ✳ a secret bake

Bridget zipped through the air, the wind whizzing her hair back and snapping her skirt against her legs as the manicured garden rushed closer.

"Bridget!" Tom screamed, flailing on the end of his elastic rope. "You're going to crash!"

"Excuse *me*," said Bridget, "I never crash!"

She pushed a button sewn into her waistband. Her paraskirt[5] deployed in an instant, and she

---

[5] A normal-seeming school skirt with a steel frame cunningly concealed in its fabric, the paraskirt enabled Bridget to float down safely from very high places — which was extremely useful for rooftop-sneaking, tree-adventuring and Miss Acrid–escaping.

floated elegantly toward the ground.

"Why couldn't you give me one of those?" muttered Tom, who was still bobbing like a broken yo-yo.

Bridget landed and smoothed her skirt.

"Because my uniform is completely unique," she said, trying, and failing, to settle her hair. "Besides, you made it down just fine."

"Just *fine*?" wailed Tom. "The first time I bounced, I thought my eyeballs were going to pop out my head!"

"Well, they didn't, did they?"

"The second time I bounced, I thought my teeth might fall out!"

"Yes," said Bridget testily, leaping to grab Tom's swinging feet, "but they—"

"The *third* time, I thought—"

"Tom Timpson! Did I not get you out of that bear trap and out of Miss Acrid's office in one piece?"

Tom landed with a thump beside a statue of a dancing dragon.

"You did," he groaned.

"Good, now get up. Quickly."

"Can't I lie here until the world stops spinning?"

"No."

"Why not?"

"Because," said Bridget, as the rope began to swing, "Miss Acrid is chasing us."

They looked up. High above, shimmying down the elastic rope, was the Mistress's unmistakably big-booted silhouette.

"*Baxter!*" she screamed. "Stay *right* there!"

"Let's go!" shouted Bridget, dragging Tom into the Great Maze.

"Wait!" said Tom. "Errant Childs get lost in there!"

"Don't be silly—I come here all the time when I'm escaping. The animals are very nice. I don't think they like Miss Acrid either."

The Great Maze was a sprawl of dense, tangled hedges, its narrow pathways full of fallen trees and out-of-control plants.

Bridget felt it wrap itself around her.

She grinned.

An owl hooted from the top of a nearby bush.

"Thank you," Bridget replied.

"What did it say?" asked Tom.

"I *think*," said Bridget, "she said we need to hurry."

Miss Acrid screamed again, and the children ran as fast as they could into the shadow of the green-smelling maze, placing their feet carefully between knotted roots and frozen puddles as Miss Acrid crunched after them.

Bridget clambered over a log beside a little pond, then reached for Tom's hand.

"Come on," she said.

"This is scary!" said Tom, glancing over his shoulder. "I think I'd rather be back in the bear trap!"

"Nonsense. Come on—sit here."

Tom sat beside the frozen water. Bubbles moved under the ice.

Invisible creatures scrattled and snuck around them, the ground hummed with the digging of frantic paws, and the hedges chirped with squirrels and birds.

Bridget closed her eyes.

"Isn't this wonderful?" she said.

"Yes," said Tom, looking around. Even the sky was hidden by the Great Maze's branches. "Are we lost?"

"Would you like to be?" asked Bridget, taking a

deep breath of cold, clean air.

"I just want to get away from Miss Acrid."

The Mistress, still three hedges distant, shrieked again.

"She'll catch us eventually, won't she?" said Tom.

"Maybe not," said Bridget. "We could keep going—anywhere we like. Anywhere in the whole world."

Tom rubbed his hands together.

"Somewhere warm, like Brazil?"

"Or Mexico."

"Japan."

"India."

"Ireland."

"Kenya."

"Australia."

"Korea."

"Canada."

Bridget sighed. "It could be nice here, you know," she said. "Sometimes I can hear the waves through the windows in our dorm."

"I've never heard them," sniffed Tom.

"That's because you always fall asleep first and you snore like a rhinoceros."

"I do not!"

"Do so."

"Do *not*!"

"Excuse *me*," said Bridget, who'd been kept awake many times by Tom's orchestral sleep-sounds. "You snore like a gigantic rhino, sleeping on its back with a heavy cold."

"Do I?"

"Yes. But I still like you."

Tom laughed.

"I wish I could be good at things, like you."

"What do you mean?"

"Oh, come on! You're good at *everything*. You can sing. You can climb on the roof. And you always, always get the better of Miss Acrid."

Bridget made a face.

"I don't think I'm really—"

"Have you ever tried something," Tom interrupted, "but found you couldn't do it?"

Bridget thought for a moment.

She'd mastered ballet in a week, and received an invitation to join the touring company of Pointe and Pirouette.[6]

She'd decided to be a detective one rainy afternoon, and solved a number of perplexing mysteries which led to the capture of a dangerous criminal.

She'd tried pottery, piano, carpentry, calligraphy, bowling, beekeeping, jigsaws, juggling, knitting and knot tying.

And done them all *perfectly*.

"It's just a matter of paying attention," she said, embarrassed. "You read the instructions, and then you do what they tell you to do."

Tom laughed.

"It's not that simple for the rest of us," he said. "Maybe one day you'll find *one* thing you're *not* good at."

"I hope not," said Bridget. "Anyway. Something I definitely *am* good at is finding things Miss Acrid doesn't want found."

She reached into her hair, fished around for a few seconds, then brought out a napkin the size of a box of matches.

---

[6] Miss Acrid ripped the invitation into tiny pieces and threw them in the bin.

"Let's have a picnic," she said, and she unfolded the napkin to reveal a small crescent of pastry.

Tom's brown eyes widened.

"What is it?"

"It's a kwassong, I think," said Bridget uncertainly, as though trying a key in an unfamiliar lock. "Mrs. Pobydd[7] made lots of them for the Families. It's a pastry."

"Like the stuff on top of an eel pie?"

"This is a different kind of pastry," said Bridget. "There aren't any eels in this one."

They listened as a pigeon flew into Miss Acrid's face.

"Told you the animals don't like her," Bridget whispered.

"So, this is a . . . cake?" said Tom.

"I don't know. But I'm pretty sure it's been baked."

"I've never had baked anything."

---

[7] Mrs. Pobydd—the Orphanage's Welsh cook—would have loved nothing more than to shower the Orphanage's one hundred and fifty-two Childs with treats and rich food, but she was just as scared of Miss Acrid as the Errant Childs were, so she reluctantly stuck to lumpy porridge and rock-hard macaroni, as instructed by the Mistress.

"Neither have I," said Bridget. She took a tiny penknife from a hidden pocket in her skirt and sliced the kwassong neatly in two. "Here you are."

"It smells lovely," said Tom.

"It does, doesn't it?" said Bridget.

She closed her eyes and let the kwassong's aroma float into her nose. It was very rich, and very buttery.

They ate in silence.

"Goodness," said Tom, licking flakes of pastry from his fingertips. "That was—"

"Wasn't it?" said Bridget.

"The crispy stuff was—"

"I know."

"And the *chewy* bits were—"

"I know!"

Bridget took a long, satisfied breath. The kwassong had washed away the poisonous taste of Miss Acrid's breakfast sandwich with such soft, velvety deliciousness her heart leaped with excitement.

In fact, she realized, she felt quite different.

Changed, somehow—as if her whole body, her whole mind, her whole *self*, had been rearranged by a few mouthfuls of kwassong.

She closed her eyes and felt its succulent warmth flow from her restless toes to the tips of her tangled hair.

She could *taste* the time and care Mrs. Pobydd had put into the baking, and she could *feel* Tom beside her—as though their hearts were connected by shimmering golden threads.

She opened her eyes, and sensed that she was someone new.

From that point on, she realized, she would understand her life as being defined by the time before the kwassong, and the time after.

She shook herself down gleefully.

Miss Acrid's footsteps had faded completely into the maze. The only sounds were the brush of reeds on the frozen pond and the distant whisper of treetop wind.

Tom sighed happily.

"Do you think all baked things are as delicious as that?" he said.

"They couldn't be," said Bridget, blinking quickly. "That was the most perfect thing I've ever eaten."

They leaned into each other, savoring the last traces of sweetness and watching ice bubbles.

A little way behind them, a clatter of branches crashed to the ground.

"I can *smell* you, *Baxter*!" Miss Acrid screamed. "You can't hide from me!"

Tom let his head fall on Bridget's shoulder.

"Why did you come and get me?" he said. "You've been so good lately. Now, when the Families come—"

"It doesn't matter about that. You're my friend and you were locked in a bear trap—of course I was going to come for you. You'd have done the same for me."

"But I'm not as brave as you, Bridget. I get so scared, and—"

"Being brave isn't about not being scared," said Bridget firmly.

A branch snapped over to their left and they heard Miss Acrid snuffling—like a hound after a scent.

"Isn't it?" whispered Tom.

Bridget shook her head.

"Being brave means doing something *even though you're scared to do it*."

"Even if it means being an Errant Child forever?"

Bridget pressed her lips tight. She took Tom's arm.

"Forever," she said.

Tom took a deep breath and held out his hand.

"Do you know what this is?" he asked.

"Of course," said Bridget. "It's the ring you were wearing when you came here."

Tom turned the ring over. Sunlight shone on its dull surface.

"It must have been my dad's," he said. "Anyway, here—I want you to have it."

Bridget leaned away.

"I couldn't," she said. "It's your *ring*! It's the most important thing to you in the whole world!"

"No, it's not," said Tom quietly, placing the ring on Bridget's palm and closing her fingers around it. "You are."

Tears sprang to Bridget's eyes.

"Goodness," she managed, as Tom slid the ring onto the thumb of her right hand, "I don't know what to say. Here—take this!"

She held out her bracelet of nano-novels.[8]

"Oh, I couldn't," said Tom. "You'd be lost without your tiny books!"

"I want you to have it!"

"But they were your *mother's*," said Tom, backing away. "I don't want to—"

"Please!" said Bridget, snapping open the clasp and pushing a little book with a red cover into his hands. "Read this, it's wonderful."

"*The Summer Book,*" said Tom, reading the spine. "What's it about?"

---

[8] A bracelet of tiny books—so small they could only be read with the aid of a magnifying glass—the nano-novels had been the only things in Bridget's possession when she'd arrived at the Orphanage as a baby.

"It's about a girl and her granny. It's so beautiful. Sophia, that's the girl's name. She loves her granny so much, and she's so happy and wild, and—"

A shadow fell over the children.

"You're going to *regret* that, *Baxter*," Miss Acrid growled.

Her nostrils billowed with wintery clouds of steam, her hair was tangled and thorny, her freezing face was stuck with feathers, and she had a twig in each ear.

"Don't you remember, Miss?" said Bridget, sucking pastry from her fingers. "You only regret the things you *don't* do."

"I'll give you something to *regret*, you *worm*!" Miss Acrid roared, grabbing them both by the collar and clomping from the maze, the Childs wriggling in her iron grip.

3

Punishment

polished pigs ✳ bird poop ✳ helter-skelter

"I trust the pigs are clean?" said Miss Acrid, from behind her enormous desk. "Underside, topside and trotter?"

Bridget set down the pig-mop and smoothed her skirt. There were flecks of mud on the hem, and her hands were red and sore.

"Yes," she said. "I polished Lord Snout till I could see my face in his bristly back."

"What about Lady Truffleton?"

"She's even shinier," said Tom.

The Mistress, the constipated, stuffed dodo peering over her shoulder, thinned her lips.

"Pond?" she snarled.

"Cleared of weeds," said Bridget, stepping away from the office's not-so-secret trapdoor.

"Lawn?"

"Flattened and cut," said Tom.

"The glasshouse?"

"Freed completely," Bridget said calmly, "from its bird-poop crust."

Miss Acrid sat back and smoothed her eyebrow. She had eaten the remainder of her breakfast sandwich and there were smudges of its fishy filling in the corners of her mouth.

"Let us recap the events of the day," she said, adjusting her medallion. "You broke into my office. You freed my prisoner. You ate my special seafood sandwich. You leaped from my window and—by forcing me to give chase—caused my hair to become entangled in the thorns of the Great Maze." She patted her hair and plucked a spike from her knuckle. "Do you think you have received fair punishment for these crimes?"

"Definitely," said Tom, stretching painfully.

Bridget thought for a moment.

"No," she said. "I think you've been horrible and mean. Like always."

Miss Acrid smiled.

"Well," she said, standing and licking away the breakfast smears. "The Families will be here soon, looking for boys and girls to *love*. All one hundred and fifty-one Errant Childs are to be lined up in the assembly hall in five minutes, with their horrid little faces *washed*, their uniforms *ironed* and their shoes *polished*."

"But, Miss Acrid," said Tom, "look how grubby we are! There's only one bath in the whole Orphanage — there's no way we'll both be ready in five minutes!"

Miss Acrid's eyes flashed, and she grinned.

Bridget squeezed Tom's hand.

"Didn't you hear her? All one hundred and fifty-*one* Childs."

Panic spread over Tom's face.

"But there's one hundred and fifty-two of us!" he cried.

"Good counting, Timpson!" snarled the Mistress, clomping round the desk and lifting Tom into the air. "One hundred and fifty-two nasty, *Errant* Childs — and yet there's only *one* who keeps filling her head with *stories* and *ideas* and *dreams*, who per*sist*ently defies me, and who re*fus*es to be squished and squashed and put in her place!" She fixed Bridget with a beady glare. "And which Child is that, I wonder?"

Bridget glared back, anger burning in the pit of her tummy.

"You're going to do it again, aren't you?" she said. "You're going to keep me away from the Families and make sure that I miss out on a *real* home."

Miss Acrid, with Tom raised and wriggling, opened her office door and gestured at the empty corridor.

Then she leaned down, so close that her fishy lips brushed the tip of Bridget's ear.

"Your choice, *Baxter*," she whispered, throwing up her not-so-secret trapdoor. The dungeon's dusty breath rushed up to meet them. "One of you gets the chance of a new *home* — the other goes into the *dun*geon!"

"Don't do it, Bridget!" shouted Tom. "This is your chance to find a *real* family!"

Bridget looked down the corridor. Any minute now, the big door would open, and the Families would wander in, hearts brimming with love.

She locked eyes with Tom.

"I love you," she said.

And jumped.

The trapdoor slammed behind her, snuffing out Tom's cries as she barreled helter-skelter into the innermost depths of the Orphanage, Miss Acrid's rancid laugh echoing around her. She landed in a heap on some ancient horse blankets, releasing a thick cloud of evil-smelling dirt.

"You're the meanest person in the world!" she shouted, brushing herself off and coughing on the dust. "You bristly old wart! You vicious old crone!"

Her voice echoed against the smooth, concrete walls.

Bridget slumped to the ground like a broken scarecrow.

I can climb out, she thought, *but by the time I do, the Families will be long gone. I'm going to be stuck as an Errant Child — again.*

The sound of running water crackled around her, punctuated by the *plink* of a distant drip.

"I'm going to make you pay, Miss Acrid," she growled, peering toward the dungeon's cavernous ceiling, beyond which lay the corridors and dorms of the Orphanage for Errant Childs. "I *swear* I'm going to make you pay!"

Then she slid to her knees, curled into a ball, and sobbed in a corner of the dungeon.

Alone.

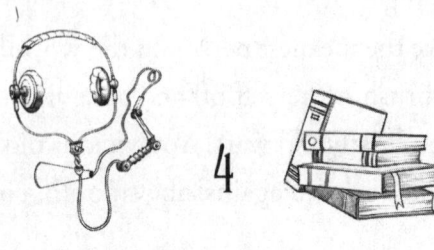

4

Alone

teeth ✳ monstrousness ✳ empty dorms

When Bridget woke an hour later, she had chewed through the cover of a nano-novel and lost the feeling in her toes.

She blinked.

The nano-novel was *A Wrinkle in Time*—one of her favorites. She closed her eyes and let its story tingle through her, a familiar vapor that put bubbles in her belly and hope in her heart.

Then she took a deep breath, opened her eyes to the dungeon's cold, empty gloom, and came back, slowly, painfully, to the Orphanage for Errant Childs.

The Families had been and gone.

Miss Acrid had won.

Bridget ran her thumb along each nano-novel's tiny spine, then shook her head.

"No," she said. "Stories aren't for telling us that monsters exist—they're to show us that monsters can be *beaten*."

She tied her hair back.

"I'm coming, Tom," she said. "Don't you worry."

Reaching into her hair, she found her Sookosocks[9] and slipped them over her boots. Then, inch by delicate inch, she began the slow climb up the helter-skelter.

Miss Acrid kept the chute's surface so well oiled that—even with the Sookosocks's incredible grip—Bridget slipped four times. Once, she tumbled all the way to the very bottom, and landed back on the dirty blankets.

But every time she fell, she got up, brushed herself down, and kept going.

On the fifth attempt, knees aching and lungs burning, her head bumped against the wooden floor

---

[9] Rubbery socks covered in a strong, waterproof adhesive which allow the wearer to remain stuck to even the slipperiest of surfaces.

of Miss Acrid's office.

This is it, she thought. *This time I'll get the best of her, once and for all.*

She thrust open the trapdoor and leaped into the room, screaming at the top of her voice.

Miss Acrid, seated behind her enormous desk, raised one half of her monobrow.

"Baxter," she said, tilting a teacup to her wicked lips. "Whatever *kept* you?"

Bridget slammed her fist in the middle of the enormous desk.

"Where's Tom?" she bellowed.

"Tom? I don't recall a *Tom*," said Miss Acrid, taking another sip. She glanced at Bridget's thumb. "What is that horrid little circle of tin, *Baxter*?"

Bridget thrust the ring under the Mistress's beak.

"It's Tom's," she said. "He *gave* it to me. That's the kind of thing you do when you love someone—something *you* would never understand."

"*Boak*," said Miss Acrid, retching dramatically. "And there's that name again—Tom. There's no *Tom* here."

"You know very well who I mean," Bridget snarled, gritting her teeth. "He's my best friend in the whole world—the one person who means more to me than anyone else."

Miss Acrid slapped her palm against her forehead.

"Of course!" she cried. "Well, you'll be *pleased* to know he's found a new family."

Bridget felt faint.

"Tom's gone?" she whispered.

"Pleasant couple," said Miss Acrid. "Dentists, of all things. Lovely teeth." She cocked her head to one side and flashed her own horsey dentistry. "I thought you'd be happy for him. After all, it was only this morning you broke into my office, freed him from the Bear Trap of Shame, desecrated my dodo and spoiled my seafood sandwich—then sacrificed yourself by *voluntarily* jumping into my dungeon. Aren't you *happy* for him?"

"You *know* I am," said Bridget, meeting the Mistress's stare head-on. "I love him."

Miss Acrid pouted.

"Then what a *shame* you won't see him again for the *rest of your life*."

Bridget felt her eyes filling up.

Don't let her see you cry, she thought.

"Where are the others?" she asked,

turning to go.

Miss Acrid drained her cup, then set it on the desk and steepled her fingers.

"Others?" she said.

"There are no 'others.'"

Bridget froze.

"What?"

"There are no Errant Childs left. Every single one of them, all one hundred and fifty-one, have gone to new families. *All of them. Every single one of them*—gone. First time it's *ever* happened—I made a *special* effort this year. Just for you."

Bridget's head spun.

"What about me?" she managed.

Miss Acrid leaned over the desk, monobrow low over her nose.

"Why, *you* get to stay for at *least* another year," she growled. "You're the last Errant Child, Baxter. But look on the bright side—there's plenty of space!"

She threw back her head and laughed her seagull's laugh.

Bridget clutched her bracelet of nano-novels.

"You're so mean," she whispered. "You're the

meanest, nastiest person in the history of everything. Meaner and nastier than anyone in any story."[10]

Miss Acrid laughed again.

"*Stories,*" she spat, as though uttering a terrible curse. "I think I'll burn those silly little books of yours—they put silly notions in your silly head!"

"Never!" shouted Bridget.

She turned and ran.

The Mistress rose to give chase, but Bridget fled through the door, leaped from the banister out onto the windowsill and scrambled up the drainpipe before the Mistress had even rounded the enormous desk.

"You can't hide forever, *Baxter*!" Miss Acrid shouted, voice ringing through the empty corridors. "It's just the two of us now—I'll get you soon enough!"

Hair billowing behind her, Bridget ran along the gutter and dropped through the window of her dormitory. The neat beds were empty, and the

---

[10] Bridget had read about lots of horrifying people, so this was quite a strong statement.

drawers hung open like the tongues of panting dogs. Empty hangers swung in the gaping wardrobe.

There wasn't an Errant Child in sight.

She really has done it, she thought, dashing through the room and peering under the beds. *She's done the cruelest thing imaginable, the cruelest thing she ever could.*

She's left me all alone.

Bridget stopped and listened to the silence.

A deep, cold dread began to fill her stomach.

She swallowed hard, tears stinging her eyes.

Running back into the corridor, she turned up the Steep Steps and burst through the library doors.

The Orphanage library was tall and vast, its bright, high windows beaming honey-sweet sunlight. Its booklined shelves were made from polished mahogany, and the floor was a mosaic of

elegant tile.[11]

Bridget took a deep breath. All around her, on teeming shelves and spinning racks, were thousands of fabulous stories—pulling at her like a powerful current.

She could *feel* the far-off lands and hidden secrets, the shadowy villains and vulgar henchmen, the valiant heroines and noble heroes, all clamoring for her attention like puppies in a pet shop window.

"When I got here, as a baby," Bridget said, taking a mop from the cupboard and filling the big, steel bucket, "the only thing I had were my mum's nano-novels. I always knew stories were important. And you've always been here for me. Whenever things seemed impossible, whenever Miss Acrid was mean, I could always come here and feel safe."

She sent a slosh of bubbly water across the floor

---

[11] Miss Acrid had accidentally made the Orphanage library very beautiful and filled it with excellent books, and—while the Mistress would never once set either of her foots inside—it was Bridget's favorite place in the whole world. Sometimes she sat in the soft chairs and read. Sometimes she wandered around, stroking the spines and murmuring the titles aloud. And sometimes she just lay on her back with books scattered over her like a blanket, and breathed in the soft, reassuring warmth of their stories.

and stepped after it, sweeping methodically under the shelves with *Schip-Schip* swoops of the ragged mop.

"Now she's done the meanest thing yet. Meaner than Moriarty, meaner than Cruella de Vil, meaner even than the Great High Witch."

She kept mopping, remembering with each *Schip* all the time she'd happily lost in this special place.

Eventually, she stepped back. The floor was gleaming like a new pin.

"Thank you, old friend," she said. "I imagine we'll be spending a lot of time together, now."

She tidied away the mop, then climbed out the library window, scrambling up the clocktower and

onto the Orphanage's highest roof. Hugging her knees and biting her lip, she stared down at the village of Belle-on-Sea, with its snow-topped spires and sparkling glass, its houses full of happiness and love.

Bridget imagined how Tom must feel—whooshing toward his new home with his new parents.

She buried her face in her hands.

"I *am* happy for you," she whispered, squeezing the ring in her fist, "of course, I am. It's just . . . this is all I have left of you."

Shadows moved under the afternoon sun as the hours slipped away. Bridget felt the clocktower's tick like a needle through the soles of her feet, and imagined her life over the next year.

The boring walks around the exercise yard—alone.

The morning gruel in the dining hall—alone.

The rainy afternoons scrubbing Lord Snout and Lady Truffleton—alone.

I'll be like a ghost, she thought. *A little ghost haunting the Orphanage.*

She pressed a handkerchief to her nose, and got ready to vanish like a puff of smoke into the winter sky.

When something moved in the distance.

Bridget reached into her hair and took out a homemade telescope.

A small green car with snow on its roof was rattling along the bumpy road toward the Orphanage gates.

"Who would be coming here?" she whispered. "At *this* time?"

A tiny flame of hope flickered in her heart.

The car bounced into the empty driveway. A small, nervous-looking man climbed out and stepped gingerly between the icy puddles.

Then he took off his hat, climbed the steps to the main entrance and rang the bell.

As though thrown by a catapult, Bridget leaped from her chimney and slid down the dining hall roof, swinging herself along the gutter, down the drainpipe and onto the chimney stack above Miss Acrid's office.

She dropped the Listening Glass into the chimney, lowered it into the

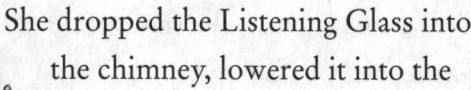

Mistress's fireplace[12] and closed her eyes.

A drumbeat of footsteps filled her ears.

"She's pacing back and forth," Bridget whispered to herself. "She only does that when she's upset."

"*Quite* unorthodox," Miss Acrid was saying. "We at the Errant Childs do *not* encourage visitation outside of—"

"I understand," the man said in a gentle voice, "but I really must speak with you."

"About what?" snapped the Mistress. Bridget heard her fingers tapping against the enormous desk.

"One of your . . . Childs. A girl."

Miss Acrid ground her teeth.

"I'm *afraid* there are no Childs left," she sneered. "None at *all*."

"But there must be," said the man, his voice

---

[12] This had to be done very carefully indeed, otherwise the glass would clatter and chime against the bricks. Miss Acrid might be monstrous and cruel and eat the world's smelliest sandwiches, but she had fantastic hearing.

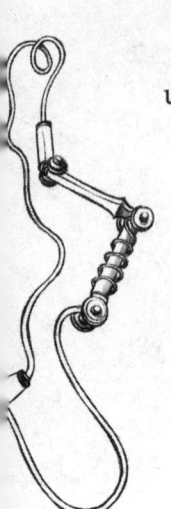

urgent. "This is a girl who's been here for a long time. She has wild hair, she loves stories, she always does the right thing, and she's terribly, terribly brave."

Bridget's heart did a somersault.

"I know of no such *child*," snarled Miss Acrid.

But there was a wobble in her voice.

"Are you sure?" said the man. "I have a name, if that would help?"

A name? thought Bridget, hardly daring to breathe.

"A name?" barked Miss Acrid.

"A name," said the man. "I saw it, written in big letters on a plaque in the hallway, over and over again. And I thought—that's her. That's the girl I'm going to look after and love for the rest of my life."

"Well?" growled the Mistress. "What *is* it? Spit it out!"

The man cleared his throat, the chair creaking as he leaned forward.

"Bridget Baxter."

5

Escape

lies ✴ the smell of cake ✴ dReams

Did he just say my name? thought Bridget.

She gripped the chimney and, pulse hammering, pressed her ear to the Listening Glass as hard as she could.

"I beg your pardon?" said Miss Acrid. Her voice had gone very quiet and thin, as though she had a pebble stuck in her throat.

"My name is Ernest Vanderpuff," said the man. "I run a business in the village—perhaps you know it?"

"We do *not* go to the . . ." Miss Acrid gagged softly, "*village*."

"Oh," said Mr. Vanderpuff. "Well, my dearest

wish in all the world is to have a child of my own to love and care for and I . . . I had a dream last night. Someone in this dream told me to come here, today. They told me there was a wild-haired, clever girl—and when I saw the name Bridget Baxter, I just *knew* that was her, and that it was me who . . . well, I'm going to look after her."

Bridget gasped.

A real home, she thought. The words felt like an explosion in her heart. She thought of her own comfortingly nonsensical dream from the night before, which had been filled with musical screaming, giant pillows and a tiny man who clapped and laughed.

Miss Acrid's fingers began to tap more quickly on the enormous desk.

"I'm afraid your *dream* was *mis*taken," she sneered. "There is nobody here by that name. There is nobody here at all, in fact—every one of our Errant Childs was taken to a new home this afternoon. *This* Orphanage is empty. Deserted. *Un*inhabited."

The explosion in Bridget's heart erupted into her hair. It stood rigidly on end, her picks and tools ringing like a forest of windblown chimes.

No! she wanted to scream. *I'm here, I'm here! Don't listen to her!*

"Are you sure?" said Mr. Vanderpuff. "My dream was really quite—"

"*Vacant,*" said Miss Acrid, who had just thought of another word. "I'm *quite* sure, yes. What kind of silly place do you think this is? We have no bats in our attics, no mouses in our walls. I'd hardly forget about a whole child, would I? Especially one as troublesome as Bridget *Baxter*."

There was a pause.

"I thought there *was* no Bridget Baxter?" said Mr. Vanderpuff.

"Exactly," said Miss Acrid.

You're so mean, Bridget thought. *The meanest meanie there ever was.*

The sun sank into the trees around the Orphanage, smothering her in the chilly cloak of evening.

"Right," said Mr. Vanderpuff. "Well . . . if there's any change to the situation, and perhaps Miss Baxter *does* arrive here—"

"You'll be the first to know," interrupted Miss Acrid. "But I can't imagine such a thing. A *dream* of all things! Nothing but figments and lies!"

Bridget pressed her ear to the Listening Glass until it grew hot and sore.

"Dreams," said Mr. Vanderpuff, making an obvious effort to compose himself, "are truthful and pure. Sometimes our dreams are all we have. In times of real hardship, when the world seems empty and cold, when we are at our most vulnerable, the most special gift is a dream filled with love."

"If you say so," Miss Acrid yawned. She let go a loud belch, then patted her stomach. "It is *dinner*time, Mr. Vandalscruff, and as I'm sure you're aware, my seafood sandwich[13] *is* waiting."

"Yes," said Mr. Vanderpuff, stepping backward. "I can smell it."

Miss Acrid clomped across the room and jerked open the door.

"Off you go, then," said the Mistress.

Bridget fed a little

---

[13] Triple-baked in Mrs. Pobydd's cast iron oven and therefore thrice as stinky, the dinnertime mackerel and cabbage cob was by far the worst of all Miss Acrid's seafood sandwiches.

more cord down the
chimney. The Listening Glass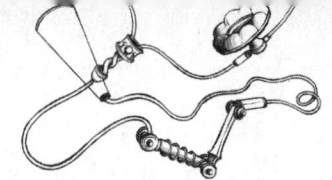
was now dangerously close to the fireplace—if
Miss Acrid glanced in that direction, she would spot
it immediately, and Bridget would lose it forever.

But it was worth the risk. She could feel it in
her hair.

Something was about to happen.

Mr. Vanderpuff's footsteps moved toward the
door.

Then he stopped and took a long, slow sniff.

"Croissants," he said, closing the door behind
him. "How lovely."

A lightning bolt shot through Bridget's body—
the same shimmering, golden connection she'd
felt between her and Tom as they'd shared the
kwassong in the maze.

He knew it just by the smell! she thought.

She heard Miss Acrid settling behind the
enormous desk, sandwich raised, and pictured the
expression of victory on her wicked face.

"All right," said Bridget, withdrawing the
Listening Glass in a single, rapid movement. "Time
to go."

Evening's cold wind grabbing at her clothes and hair, she scrambled to the very top of the chimney pot, closed her eyes and pinched her nose.

Then dropped.

She landed in a puff of billowing soot, throwing clouds of coal dust over Miss Acrid's hideous things.

"Wha-wha-whAAAAAT?" shrieked the Mistress, waving blindly as she staggered through the murk. "What's happened? Where's my—?"

"Why did you lie?" growled Bridget.

Miss Acrid froze. Bridget's voice seemed to have come from everywhere and nowhere all at once.

The Mistress's sharp little ears swiveled swiftly.

"Baxter?" she said, taking a cautious clomp through the gloom. "Is that you?"

"Why did you *lie*?" Bridget growled again, knocking a jar of eyeballs from the mantlepiece.

It shattered on the floor.

Miss Acrid arrived in a swirl of dust to find Bridget had vanished, leaving the rolling, blurping eyeballs staring up from the carpet.

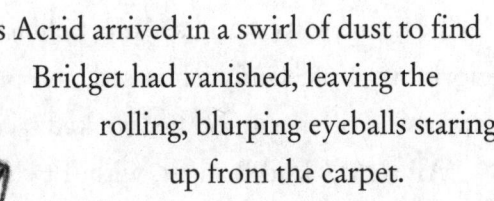

"You're making a mistake going up against *me*, *Baxter*," said the Mistress, pacing along the wall. "All the womans in my family—right back to my great-great-great-great-great-great-great-great-great-grandmama—are as strong as oxes."

"You don't scare me," said Bridget. "Not anymore. Someone's come for me. I'm leaving."

Miss Acrid grabbed at empty space.

"Pah!" she said. "You don't deserve a new home. You don't deserve *love*."

"Everyone deserves love," said Bridget, right behind her.

A big, ugly vase shattered against the wall.

Miss Acrid spun around.

"Not naughty childs," she said, grabbing once more at thin air. "Naughty childs, noisy childs, childs who are full of ideas and opinions and dreams deserve to be shut away. That stupid Vandalscruff is gone forever and there's nothing—you—can—do—about—it!"

She hopped forward, snatching at nothing and

landing on her knees.

"The word," yelled Bridget, appearing right in front of her, "is *children*!"

And she shoved the disgusting seafood sandwich in Miss Acrid's astonished mouth.

"*Mmmmmff!*" screamed the Mistress.

"You mustn't speak with your mouth full," said Bridget, leaping onto the enormous desk. Then she added, "Fish face."

And jumped out the window.

She fell, arms wide, into the sharp whip of wind—so happy, so distractedly gleeful with the joy of *finally* escaping, that she didn't notice Tom's ring had slipped from her thumb on her way down the chimney.

Her uniform snapped against her legs as she zoomed, eyes watering, through the tops of the trees. She watched the towers of the Orphanage disappear behind her, then focused on the road that led to Belle-on-Sea.

And the little green car puttering along it.

"Goodbye, Miss Acrid!" she shouted. "Goodbye,

Orphanage for Errant Childs!"

She deployed her paraskirt with a *whump* that stopped her in midair, mere inches from the car's front window, then landed lightly on the roof.

"Argh!" cried Mr. Vanderpuff, swerving off the road in fright. "What on earth is—?"

Bridget tapped the passenger window.

Mr. Vanderpuff wound it down, and Bridget dropped neatly into the passenger seat.

"Where did—? Who are—?" spluttered Mr. Vanderpuff.

Bridget wiped soot from her eyes and shook out her hair in a big, orange cloud.

"Hello," she said. "I'm Bridget Baxter."

6
Miss Acrid Gives Chase

explosion ✶ steam-powered roller skates ✶ goodbye, Sherlock

Mr. Vanderpuff was struggling to control the car.

"How in the world did—?" he spluttered. "What are you—? You landed on—!"

"It's a paraskirt," said Bridget, smoothing the fabric over her knees. "A simple matter of physics."

"*Simple* matter?"

"Absolutely," said Bridget. "But that's the least of our worries."

"Is it? I should think that—"

"Please, Mr. Vanderpuff, pay attention! Miss

Acrid will certainly have started giving chase by now—we need to get beyond the gates, or we're done for!"

"Miss Acrid is *what*?" cried Mr. Vanderpuff, grabbing hold of his rearview mirror.

"Giving chase," said Bridget again, speaking as clearly as she could, "and getting closer and closer and closer and closer. She won't go beyond the Orphanage gates—she never does—but if she catches us before that, I have a nasty feeling it'll be something worse than the dungeon—for both of us! Now, what do you see in the mirror?"

"Nothing! I . . ." Mr. Vanderpuff's eyebrows shot up. "Oh."

"Miss Acrid?" said Bridget.

"Yes!"

"Mouth open and screaming at the top of her voice?"

"Yes!"

"Waving a sword shaped like a salmon?"

"I hardly think she'd have a . . . wait . . . yes!"

"And is she wearing gigantic roller skates shaped like steam trains, with tiny chimneys and puffs of smoke and everything?"

"How do you—? Yes! Yes, all of that!"¹⁴

"Then let's get rid of her!" said Bridget, poking her head out the sunroof.

Mr. Vanderpuff jumped on the accelerator, and the little car shot down the hill toward the Orphanage's big, iron gates.

Miss Acrid hurtled toward them, salmon-sword flying, hair wild and swirling, moving so quickly the tip of her nose was starting to glow red.

"You're coming back with me, gal!" screamed the Mistress, her steam-powered roller skates creating a frantic *chuff-chuff-chuff*. "You're ERRANT! You'll never escape!"

One of the roller skates gave a *toot*.

Bridget shot the Mistress a wide smile, then popped her head inside the car.

"You don't have any anti-tank equipment in here, do you?"

"Anti-*tank*?"

"Yes!"

---

¹⁴ This was how Miss Acrid *always* gave chase.

"Of *course* not! What for?"

"These are very *large* roller skates, Mr. Vanderpuff," said Bridget. "What about a torch?"

Mr. Vanderpuff started rummaging in the car's glove box.

"There's a map, an apple core, some fluff . . ."

Bridget stood up. Mr. Vanderpuff swerved to avoid a startled rabbit, and Bridget gripped the sides of the car.

"Keep us steady!" she shouted.

"I'm trying!" Mr. Vanderpuff shouted back. "You need to sit down—this isn't safe!"

"Won't be a moment!"

Miss Acrid had closed the gap to a couple of meters—Bridget could smell the puffs of roller-skate smoke and see the anger dancing in the Mistress's eyes. A terrified badger was spread-eagled against her belly, pinned there by the incredible speed.

Miss Acrid grinned,

showing yellow teeth stuck with high-speed flies.

"I've got you!" she growled, as the badger slid off and scampered into the bushes. "You're *mine*, Baxter, *mine!*"

Bridget gripped her bracelet of nano-novels and looked at the title between her thumb and forefinger.

"*The Hound of the Baskervilles,*" she whispered, unclipping the brass clasp. "You've got me through some tough times, Sherlock. I read you in the dungeon. I read you on the roof. You gave me lots of ideas for cunning escapes. And now I need one last favor."

"Nearly . . . there . . ." grunted Miss Acrid, fingertips touching the little car.

"No," said Bridget, "you're not."

And she tossed the tiny *Hound of the Baskervilles* into the chimney of Miss Acrid's left roller skate—where it stuck.

Bridget dropped into the passenger seat and strapped herself in.

The chuff-chuff-chuff of the roller skates had been replaced by a high-pitched whine, as of a kettle coming to the boil.

"What have you done?" screamed Miss Acrid, wobbling as her roller skate swelled like a balloon.

"*BaxTERRRRRRRRRRRAAAAAAAAAA—ARGH!*"

"Let's go!" yelled Bridget, as Mr. Vanderpuff screeched round the final corner and through the towering gates.

The roller skate exploded, sending a shower of sparks and flames into the night sky.

Bridget glanced in the rear-view mirror as the little car sped toward Belle-on-Sea and saw the Mistress sitting in the middle of a soot-black circle, shaking her fist in a dizzy, lopsided way.

"What did you *do*?" said Mr. Vanderpuff, his knuckles white on the steering wheel.

Bridget looked innocently out the window.

"I just gave her something to read," she said.

Part Two
Candlewick Place

A New Home

Vanderpuff's Bake Shop ✳ Belle-on-Sea ✳ Signs

Rattling and hopping and generally seeming that it might collapse at any second, the little green car pulled into the curb and stopped with a soft, happy *clunk*.

Mr. Vanderpuff switched off the engine, then returned his hands to the steering wheel.

"I haven't quite recovered from that," he said.

Bridget took a deep inhalation. The old car smelled fabulous: the rich sweetness of the sagging leather seats, the rubbery smell of the mats, and something else—something lovely, that she couldn't quite place. She pressed her nose to the window.

"Hasn't anyone dropped in through your car window, then blown up a steam-powered roller skate before?" she said.

"No," said Mr. Vanderpuff carefully, his hands still gripping the steering wheel, which had bent slightly in his grip. "No, they haven't. That was, in fact, my first-ever car chase."

"*Oh*," said Bridget.

"Will she keep coming after us? Miss Acrid, I mean."

"No," said Bridget firmly. "I told you—she won't follow us through the gates. She never leaves the grounds of the Orphanage for Errant Childs."

Mr. Vanderpuff released a long, slow exhalation.

"Good," he said. "Well, we're here."

"Where is here?"

"Outside my shop on Candlewick Place, in the village of Belle-on-Sea."

Bridget wound down her window. The moon was rising behind the clocktower's corkscrew steeple, bathing the street in cool, milky light. All the buildings were old-fashioned and handsome, with polished doors, crisscross patterns on the windows, and the warm, wintery glow of candles. The whole *street*, she realized, was glowing with a well-built, luxurious happiness, as though lit from within. Bridget took a deep breath and let the village's sweet air of frost, pencil shavings and honeysuckle fill her chest.

She had never experienced anything like it.

Imagine living in a place like this, she thought. *A happy, safe, pretty place. A place without dungeons or fishy sandwiches. Where you don't get woken in the middle of the night to scrub floors, or get chased with swords shaped like fish.*

"It looks very nice," she said aloud.

"Thank you," said Mr. Vanderpuff, streetlight flickering on his caramel skin. "I've been very happy here. I hope you will be, too."

"Who told you about me?" she asked. "In your dream."

Silence fell on the car like a blanket. It seemed to snuff out the light, leaving the space between them airless and cold.

Mr. Vanderpuff smiled, and the moment lifted.

"I didn't realize you'd heard that," he said.

An elderly couple walked past, arm in arm. The lady raised her umbrella in greeting, and Mr. Vanderpuff nodded back.

"I heard everything," said Bridget, wrapping her arms around her knees and settling into the passenger seat. "Miss Acrid lied and said I didn't exist, then sneered at your dream. I don't want you to feel bad about that. She's the meanest person in the world."

Mr. Vanderpuff laughed.

"Thank you, Bridget. I really treasure my dreams. Don't you?"

"Of course! Even the silly ones. Last week I dreamed the mice elected me Mayor of Mousetown[15] and gave me a tall hat made of cheese. Who told you about me, in your dream?"

Mr. Vanderpuff nodded.

"You like to ask questions, don't you?"

"Very much."

Mr. Vanderpuff lowered his head.

---

[15] Bridget's first act as mayor had been to invite the cats to a traditional Mousetown tea party, to help everyone make friends and play nicely. Afterward, everyone ate her hat.

"It was my wife, Etta. She told me there was a lovely, brave girl who needed rescuing, and that I'd find her in the Orphanage for Errant Childs."

"She was mostly right."

"Oh?"

"She was right that I was in the Orphanage. I've been there my whole life. And I am brave."

"Then how was she wrong?"

"Because I never need rescuing—I rescue myself. One time, Miss Acrid locked me in a *suitcase*, threw me in the lake, and I still got out in time for games."

"A suitcase?"

"A red one," said Bridget seriously.

"Well, that's very impressive," said Mr. Vanderpuff. "But everyone needs rescuing, sometimes. It doesn't matter how clever we are, or how brave. Etta also said that you had lots of wonderful hair, and that you asked lots of questions."

Bridget pulled her hair high over her head, then let it fall back down.

"My hair ate a comb once," she said. "Then it burped."

Mr. Vanderpuff raised his eyebrows.

"I've never been fond of burps," he said. "Let's try and keep those to a minimum."

"Is Etta waiting for us in the shop?" asked Bridget, who liked burping very much indeed.

The moon disappeared behind a cloud.

"No," said Mr. Vanderpuff, climbing out of the little green car. "Come on, it's getting late."

Wooden signs swung melodically outside each shop on Candlewick Place: a sharpened pencil for the stationer, a feathered hat for the milliner, a flowing flower for the florist.[16]

Bridget smoothed her paraskirt and followed Mr. Vanderpuff.

Painted in gold across the shining door and polished window of his shop was the word:

[16] There was even a sign-shaped sign outside the sign maker's shop.

She squinted up at the silhouette of the sign hanging over their heads. It had a curved shape, like a crescent moon.

She'd been so sure the kwassong was a sign.

And there it is, she thought, *it's the sign outside Mr. Vanderpuff's shop!*

Mr. Vanderpuff opened the door, releasing a whoosh of sweetness and sugar.

"Welcome," he said, "to Vanderpuff's Bake Shop."

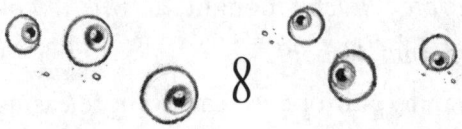

8

Miss Acrid's Discovery

badger stink ✳ rage ✳ a precious thing

The door creaked open. Miss Acrid—face scorched, hair frazzled, reeking of badger—squelched awkwardly inside. She was soaked to the bone[17] and waddled like a wooden doll—arms out, legs straight—trying to keep her freezing wet clothes as far from her skin as possible.

She muttered as she picked her way through the debris of Bridget's escape: the dunes of chimney soot,

---

[17] Mrs. Pobydd had hosed her down with freezing-cold water, something the cook would remember happily for the rest of her life.

rolling eyeballs, smashed vases and spoiled seafood sandwiches.

So much had been broken.

And Miss Acrid's mind had snapped.

She looked at the mess, a snarl on her fishy lips. Her eyebrow crunched in the middle.

Gripped by white-hot fury, she raised her salmon-sword — and swung.

"*Curse* every car and croissant!" she shrieked, shattering a plate of cakes.

"*Curse* all the badgers and books!" she barked, batting books from the shelf.

"*Curse* the Childs!" she howled, scudding her stuffed dodo on the beak. "Curse ALL the Childs! Every stinking *one of them*!"

The dodo spun on one foot — then toppled into a puddle of eyeballs.

Miss Acrid, buoyed by volcanic rage, swung the salmon-sword until all that remained of her office was a cloud of dust and splinters. Every stick of furniture, every pane of glass, every last one of her hideous things, lay in pieces around her.

"And most of all," panted Miss Acrid, chewing some fish she'd found between her teeth, "curse that little wretch... ingrate... devil! It's all *her* fault! She *made* me do it—made me send *all* of them to *loving families*." Miss Acrid recoiled as though she'd caught the smell of dog poo on her shoe. "And now my precious Orphanage is done for!"

She listened to the corridors. Silent and empty— empty of the rancid Childs that had been *hers* to squash like bugs. The Orphanage had been a great wind-up toy, *her* toy, and *Baxter* had stolen the key.

A flame erupted in the Mistress's belly.

"*GAAAAAAAAH!*" she screamed, kicking open the window.

She pointed her fist at the rooftops of Belle-on-Sea and shook it as hard as she could.

"Curse you a *thousand times*, Bridget *Bax*ter! May your shoelaces snap! May your milk turn *lumpy* and *sour*! May your socks be forever mismatched! May your bed be full of farty hedgehogs! May the skies rain on your *rot*ten face, and your—"

Her toe nudged something with a *clink*.

She looked down.

A shiny loop of metal was poking out from the rubble and clutter.

"Hellooooo," she whispered. "What have we here?"

Kneeling, she blew away the soot and fluff—to reveal a small, silver ring.

"*Tom Timpson's* ring." She grinned, a wicked light in her eyes.

She turned and laughed her maniacal-seagull laugh out the window, the ring clutched in her grubby paw.

"Oh, I've got you now, *Baxter*!" she cried. "I've got you now!"

9

Room of Bed

waking up ✳ Pascal La Fleur ✳ sentient bedclothes

Bridget opened her eyes and enjoyed the befuddled, blissful swirl of waking up naturally.

It was the first time in her life she hadn't been woken by the Orphanage's shrieking bell.

After years in a dormitory of snoring, coughing, muttering, sneezing, farting Childs, the sheer force of the quiet was overwhelming.

The last traces of Bridget's dreams, where she was flying beside badgers and swimming with salmon, floated away . . . and she found herself staring at an elaborate, decorative ceiling.

She sniffed. The air smelled of lavender and cream. Bridget sat bolt upright.

"I really *am* here!" she cried, flopping back into bed. "Let's see . . . I remember escaping from Miss Acrid, then we arrived in the village and walked into the shop . . . into the *bakery*! And that wonderful smell!"

Bright ribbons of excitement wrapped around Bridget as she recalled the bakery aroma shooting out the door and into her tummy.

"I'm in Vanderpuff's Bake Shop! And I . . . I . . . goodness me," she gasped, wriggling under the covers. "I've never . . . been so . . . *comfortable*!"

She squirmed farther into the fluffy warmth, which cocooned around her.

All that could be seen, amid the cloud of comfortable covers, was her thicket of hair.

"*Mmmmfffflllll*," said Bridget.[18]

Time slowed down as she drifted on currents of snoozy comfort, her muscles all floopy and soft.

She had never experienced anything like it.

---

[18] The Orphanage beds were hard as bricks, the unsmooshy pillows grimly thin, and the "feather" covers were just that—covers which contained a single feather.

Something landed beside her head.

Bridget froze.

"What on earth . . . ?" said a tiny, high-pitched voice. "Who left all this hair lying around?"

Bridget peered through her fringe.

A tiny man was examining a strand of her hair. He was the size and shape of a cabbage, his bright, confused face glowing under a tall white hat. A long, curled moustache stuck out like whiskers from under his nose.

He dropped the hair and shook his head.

"What a mess," he said.

"Ahem," said Bridget.

"Aaah!" screamed the little man, falling backward with a whirr of his tiny arms.

With tremendous effort, Bridget lifted her head an inch from the pillow. The man was rolling away, his eyes wide with shock.

"A girl!" he shrieked, then, as realization dawned, he added, "Bless my sieve—you can *see* me?"

"Of course," said Bridget, propping herself up on her elbows. "Am I not supposed to?"

"How *wonderful*!" the little man cried. He rocked himself to his feet and rushed forward, beaming, taking Bridget's hand in his miniature grip. "How *wonderful*! My name is Pascal La Fleur. Oh, I can't believe I'm going to have . . . that there's someone, *anyone*, who . . ."

Pascal's face began to redden.

"Nice to meet you, Mr. La Fleur—I'm Bridget Baxter," said Bridget, rubbing her hand. Pascal was small, but he was extremely strong. "Um . . . are you all right?"

"Yes!" wailed Pascal, as tears exploded from his eyes. "Oh, blast my silly tears—but it's such fabulous news! Things aren't as they should be and, of course, I'm the bakery's elf! I'm *meant* to make it right—but I *can't*! I've tried *everything* and the door just *won't open*!"

"There, there," said Bridget, cuddling Pascal as he snorted and sniffed. It was like hugging a very small, very squeezy football. "Which door won't open?"

"The Locked and Secret Door!" howled Pascal.

"Well," said Bridget, rummaging in her hair until she found a handkerchief. "Why don't you speak to Mr. Vanderpuff?"

Pascal wiped his eyes. The handkerchief looked like a blanket in his hands.

"He can't see me!" he cried. "Every elf's greatest wish is to be seen by their shopkeeper—Gracie in the grocer's sleeps in her mistress's bed—but Mr. Vanderpuff hasn't been able to see me for years. And now I think . . . I think he's forgotten I exist!"

Bridget patted the little man's back as he honked more tearful bogeys into her handkerchief.

"Why can't he see you?" she asked.

Pascal tilted his head.

"Don't you *know*?"

"Nope," said Bridget. "We didn't have elves in the Orphanage."

"The orphana . . ." Pascal dabbed at his nose. "Well, an elf can only be seen by their shopkeeper when the shop is a happy, busy, thriving place."

"Oh," said Bridget, taken aback. "Isn't the bake shop busy, then?"

Pascal laughed.

"Of course it is!"

"Then isn't Mr. Vanderpuff happy?"

"He is, he is . . ." said the elf, wringing his hands. "And he's the loveliest man you could ever wish to meet. But it's like . . . there's a part of him missing—the part that would allow him to feel magic in the world."

"Why don't we try again?" said Bridget. "I'll come with you. We can talk to him together."

Pascal's smile dropped and he looked, in an instant, almost unbearably sad.

"I *do* try," he said. "I can't tell you how many times I've held on to his coffee cup, or jumped up and down on his mixing table, or passed him the soap in the bath . . . but whenever he looks at me, he tells himself he's seeing things. 'I must be tired' he'll say, or 'too much coffee again, Ernest!' As if I'm just a figment of his imagination!"

He blew his nose with a loud *honk*.

Bridget shifted under his weight.

"But you saw me," said the elf, "as soon as you laid eyes on me. That's *very* special." He looked at Bridget, his eyes sparkling. "Are you a witch?"

Bridget thought for a moment.

"I don't think so," she said. "I just see what's in

front of me."[19]

Pascal's eyes flashed.

"*Very* clever," he said. "Tell me, do you like exploring?"

"I *love* exploring!" said Bridget. "I was the only one brave enough to go into the Orphanage's attic, and the first person *ever* to map out the Great Maze."

Pascal hopped from her lap and held out his arm.

"Then we, Bridget Baxter, are going to have a *super* time!"

Bridget linked her pinkie through his elbow.

"All right," she said, sitting up properly. "I'll get dressed, and then—*aaaargh!*"

The covers had reached out with soft, powerful arms and grabbed her back into their cozy folds.

Bridget blinked, bewildered, from inside them.

"What's happening?" she asked.

"Of course!" said Pascal, slapping his forehead as though he'd forgotten something important.

---

[19] In fact, though she didn't know it, Bridget's great-great-great-grandmother Bridgette, *had* been a witch. She lived in a windmill in France, where she spent her long and happy life collecting wildflowers, delivering babies and telling other people what to do.

"He's got you some of Mrs. MacGlover's Sentient Covers!"[20]

"Sentient? As in a mind of their own?"

"Oh, yes," said Pascal, "and they don't want you to get up yet."

"They don't?" said Bridget, tensing her muscles. "Then what do I do?"

Pascal gave her an extensive, facial shrug.

"Have another little snooze?" he said.

Bridget tried to leap to her feet, but the covers pulled her back in again and wrapped her in smooshy tentacles of feathery fluff.

"*Right . . .*" she said, blowing her fringe from her eyes and trying to wrestle free, "well, I *have* to get up, so you—have—to—let—me—go!"

The covers—strong as a bear and soft as a duckling's belly—shifted slightly and strengthened their gentle grip.

Pascal was chuckling kindly, hands resting on his

---

[20] Mrs. MacGlover's Sentient Covers™ are extremely special, each having their own personality. They are also very rare—they can be made only in the village of Belle-on-Sea, and only during the thirteen days before the Night of the Hungry Ghosts (when ghosts walk the earth, snacking as they please).

spherical tummy.

"You're wasting your time there," he said, with a yawn. "Maybe we *should* just have another snooze."

"But I want to get up and explore!" shouted Bridget. She grabbed a fistful of covers and held them up. "If you won't listen to me, maybe you'll listen to the meanest, scariest person in the whole world!"

She took a deep breath.

"You might want to protect your ears, Pascal."

"If you say so," yawned Pascal, pressing his tiny fingers in his tiny ears.

"*Aaaaaalll right, you silly COVERS!*" Bridget shrieked, in perfect imitation of Miss Acrid. "You let me *GO* this very *INSTANT*—or I'll have you sliced up and made into *handkerCHIEFS!*"

The covers did not move—they simply rumbled. Bridget had the feeling that they were laughing.

"Goodness," she said.

She wriggled and kicked—but the covers just snuggled her in even closer, and Bridget felt herself drifting back to sleep like a twig caught in a powerful tide.

Sensing their advantage, the covers curled

Bridget into the most comfortable position she had ever known, turning her into a kind of weightless, floating starfish.

"Comfy?" asked Pascal, between snores.

"Yeah . . ." mumbled Bridget, drool glistening at the corner of her mouth. "Mibbeyourright . . . mibbeanotherfew . . . minnitswouldn—no!"

She blinked quickly and shook her head.

"I have to get up! I—*want* to—get up—I–" The comfort increased. "I—I have to—go to the bathroom!"

The covers shrank back in an instant, leaving Bridget fighting fresh air.

She landed on Pascal with a *splat*.

"You're up, then?" chuckled the elf.

Bridget rolled her eyes.

"You could have *told* me those were the magic words," she said, picking him up. It was like lifting a small bag of sand.

"I said we're going to have *fun*," said Pascal, with a wink. "Wasn't it more fun working it out for yourself?"

"I suppose so," said Bridget. "Yes, it was."

Now that the covers were lifeless and flat, she

saw for the first time that there was no floor in the room at all, no carpet or tile or wood to be seen. And there was no furniture either—just a lot of drawers and doors set into the walls.

The whole room—back-to-back and side-to-side—was bed.

"Goodness," she said, dressing quickly in her old uniform. It was tricky to balance on a room-sized mattress, and she fell over more than once, much to Pascal's amusement.

"That's a splendid bruise on your elbow," he said.

"Bashed it on the dungeon's helter-skelter," said Bridget, glancing down.

"The graze on your knee?"

"Broken roof tile."

"Cut on your forehead?"

"Landed in a tree."

Pascal puffed out his cheeks.

"Good heavens," he said.

Bridget checked the lockpicks in her hair, patted the inventions in her pockets, and held her nano-novels close to her heart. Everything was in order.

Until she looked at her right hand.

"Oh, *no*!" she wailed.

"What?" asked Pascal.

"Tom's ring!" cried Bridget. "It's gone! I must have dropped it during the car chase! Unless it's lost in all this bed . . . um, excuse me, Covers?"

The covers rippled.

"Is there a ring, wrapped up in you somewhere? It's small and silver, and means more to me than anything in the whole world."

Waves rippled here and there on the surface of the bed, and Bridget realized the covers were looking for Tom's ring, like a dog after a scent.

After a minute or so, the covers gave a final, tiny puff.

"It's all right," said Bridget, sadness settling heavily in her tummy. "Thank you for checking."

I'm sorry, Tom, she thought. *I can't believe I lost the last thing I have to remember you by.*

She felt as though she might cry, so gave herself a shake.

"Right," she said aloud. "This isn't just a bedroom— it's a whole room of bed! I know how to make a bed, but how do you make a whole bed-room?"

"By yourself?" said Pascal, climbing on to the

windowsill and giving her a broad grin.

Bridget narrowed her eyes at him, then smiled.

"Are all elves as cheeky as you?" she asked, starting at one corner of the massive bed.

"Oh, yes," said Pascal. "Giving cheek is an important elf tradition!"

"It's one of my traditions, too," said Bridget, pulling the Sentient Covers until they were flat and smooth. "Do all shops have elves, then?"

Pascal nodded.

"Everywhere that makes or sells things," he said. "Shoemakers, florists, chandlers—"

"Is that someone who makes candles?" said Bridget.

"That's right! Chandlers' elves are called Waxers. Florist elves are called Blooms, mechanical elves are called Greasers—"

"What are baking elves called?" asked Bridget.

Pascal puffed out his chest.

"Butters," he said proudly.

"And you do lots of little jobs?"

"Yes, indeed," said Pascal. "Tidying up, obviously, getting things ready for the morning, making sure everything the master needs is readily available—"

"And do you ever, you know, hide things?"

Pascal looked around uneasily.

"What do you mean?" he said.

"Well," said Bridget, "I mean, like his house keys, or his favorite hat or something. Just so he has to rummage around in a panic for five minutes."

Pascal couldn't help himself—he burst out laughing, his hands clasped to his tummy.

"Yes! How did you know? We elves call that 'Hideys.' It's a favorite elf pastime—very traditional."

Bridget walked to the opposite corner ("Twelve steps!" she said to Pascal) and pulled the covers tight. It was hard work, and she paused to wipe sweat from her brow.

Eventually, the whole Room of Bed was made—neat as a pin.

"Good day, Covers," said Bridget.

The covers rippled like a pond.

Pascal climbed up her leg and settled on her shoulder.

"Lovely job," he said. "You're very good at making beds."

Bridget nodded. She rubbed the thumb on her

right hand and took a deep breath.

"Thank you," she said, thinking of what Tom had said in the Great Maze. "I'm good at lots of things."

"Such as?"

"Oh, handstands, hula-hooping, solving mysteries. Who do you think found the Long-lost Eyebrows of the Orphanage Statue, or the Legendary Tuck Shop of the Errant Childs?[21] And now, my new elf friend, I'm going to do the thing I do best of all."

Pascal clapped his hands.

"And what is that?" he asked, as Bridget walked into the corridor and inhaled the great, billowing sugar-cloud of Vanderpuff's Bake Shop.

She grinned.

"Be nosey and explore."

---

[21] Bridget, of course.

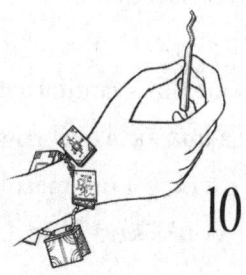

10

The Locked and Secret Door

the bakery ✳ temptation resisted ✳ a golden whisk

The sweet, bakery aroma intensified as they moved toward the stairs — a warm smell that was rich and buttery and mouth-wateringly, tooth-achingly, tummy-rumblingly delicious.

"Oh, my," said Bridget, breathing deeply.

"I know," said Pascal. "It's almost like you can taste it through your nose."

Beneath Bridget's feet ran a shiny wooden floor, the edges of its polished boards rising against her stockinged soles. There was a grandfather clock beside her bedroom door, and lots of paintings on the wall. A bristly velvet chair stood beside the telephone at the top of the twirly staircase, its seat lit by a stained-glass lamp.

"There's something about this grandfather clock," she said, examining it with a quizzical eyebrow. "Like it's more than just a clock, if you get my meaning."

"You are sharp, aren't you?" said Pascal. "All in good time, I'm sure."

"All right," said Bridget.

She studied the paintings as she moved toward the stairs. There were landscapes of sunshine and lightning—all vivid skies and jagged mountains—and lots of animals: galloping horses, migrating ducks and poker-playing dogs.[22]

And there was an empty space, as sudden and vacant as a missing tooth. The thin, rectangular shadow of a frame was ghosted on the wall, and Bridget's fingertips found the tiny hole left by the picture hook.

"Why has this painting been taken down?" she asked.

"I'm not sure," said Pascal, suddenly shifty.

---

[22] Playing cards is very hard for dogs, because their wagging tails betray their good hands. Only the very *best* poker-hounds make it into the paintings.

"You're not going to tell me?"

The elf pretended to examine his fingernails.

"Fine," said Bridget. "I shall discover all the secrets here, in time—I'm *very* good at finding out secrets."

She climbed onto the banister.

"Ready?" she asked.

"Of course!" said Pascal, gripping his hat.

"Then off we go!" cried Bridget, sliding past the frescoes of breads and cakes that twirled beside the twirly stairs.

She landed, silent as a cat, in the downstairs hall. The aroma had grown even more intense.

Bridget found herself drooling.

"Where is Mr. Vanderpuff?" she asked.

"He'll be in the shop," said Pascal. "This is right in the middle of the morning rush."

"What's a 'morning rush'?"

"The busiest part of the morning!" said Pascal, beaming. "When all of Belle-on-Sea come for the day's bakes and cakes."

"I see," said Bridget, who'd never been in any kind of shop before. "How exciting." She looked at the three large doors in front of her.

The sign on the door to the right read: SHOP
The sign on the door to the left read: BAKERY
And the sign on the middle door read: SECRET

"Oh, good," said Bridget, grinning. "A *mystery*."

Pascal nodded.

"This is the door I was telling you about," he said, "the one that just won't open."

Bridget thought about the lockpicks hidden in her hair.

"For now," she said, approaching the Locked and Secret Door.

The doors to the bakery and shop were painted, like the ones upstairs, a lovely deep green. But the Locked and Secret Door was made of dark, heavy wood, and secured by iron hinges and iron locks. The round, iron handle—almost as big as Bridget's head—had the outline of a golden whisk carved into its surface.

"*Very* mysterious," said Bridget.

She pressed her cheek to the wood. It hummed gently, and she had the sense of something almost *glowing* on the other side.

She sat back on her haunches.

"Well," she said happily, "this is *very* mysterious indeed."

She reached into her hair.

"What are you doing?" asked Pascal.

"I'm going to try and open it," said Bridget, withdrawing the curly-tip pick and sliding it into the massive keyhole.

Pascal shook his head sadly.

"Mr. V has had any number of locksmiths try their luck," he said. "He had lumberjacks try to smash their way in with axes and fire. He even hired a thief, once—a man who'd been in prison for breaking into banks and vaults—but the lock hasn't budged an inch. It's hopeless, I'm afraid."

Bridget frowned. She rummaged in her hair, took out the tweezle-tip and tried again.

But no matter which of the picks she tried, there came no sound, no whisper, no little voice speaking through the tips of her fingers.

The Locked and Secret Door was silent and still, its great lock unyielding.

"Oh," she said.

"I told you," said Pascal. "Come on, I'll show you the bakery."

Bridget looked at the golden whisk. Walking away from a job unfinished—a challenge unconquered—was deeply unsettling.

Tom's voice echoed in her head: *Maybe one day you'll find one thing you're not good at.*

"I'm coming back," she told the Locked and Secret Door. "I'll get you open—don't worry about that."

She pushed at the door to the bakery.

The room was large and white, with a vaulted ceiling covered in white tiles. Everything was bright and clean. There were tottering towers of bowls, silvery spoons and hulking mixers. Tiny bottles of colored liquids were lined like soldiers on every shelf. The whole place had a sense of busy purpose. It was a place where things were made.

"I've never been in a bakery before," said Bridget. "It's lovely."

"It's more than that," said Pascal, beaming wide-eyed around him. "It's magical."

"Will Mr. Vanderpuff let *me* help?"

"Of *course*, he will!" cried Pascal. "I'm quite sure that's why you're here—to help him run the bake shop!"

Bridget's heart leaped.

"I'd love that!" she said. "Can we see the shop now?"

"Let's," said Pascal, rubbing his hands together. "Just you wait."

Bridget went into the hallway, past the mystery door with its golden whisk, and pushed the door to the shop.

She stopped in her tracks.

Her mouth fell open. She stared.

"I *know*," whispered Pascal.

"Pascal," Bridget whispered back, "this is the most wonderful place I've ever seen in my whole life."

Mr. Vanderpuff's shop was *beautiful*: ceiling-high shelves trimmed with shining gold; high-mirrored walls with ladders on wheels; a gleaming glass cabinet as

long as the room, topped by a brass till as tall and ornate as a wedding cake.

Every surface *teemed* with breads and pastries and cakes—each elegant morsel marked with a pretty label.

There were customers queuing at the counter, all wearing the same rapt expression.

Bridget breathed in and closed her eyes, letting herself be filled with the air's aromatic symphony: the *ting* of lavender, the *snap* of strawberries, the *whoosh* of fresh bread, the *pop* of buttercream and, above and around it all, the deep *boom* of chocolate.

Vanderpuff's wasn't just a bakery—it was an orchestra of sugary wonder.

Pascal nudged her ear. Bridget reached up and held his hand.

"My usual, Mr. Vanderpuff!" exclaimed a large, red-faced man in a porkpie hat.

"A baker's dozen, Mr. Constantine?"[23] replied Mr. Vanderpuff's kindly voice from somewhere beyond

---

[23] Mr. Constantine was the stationer on Candlewick Place. He was permanently doused in a blossom of wood shavings and smelled sweetly of pencils.

the queue.

"And throw in a couple of Caramagnificent Donuts," said Mr. Constantine. "It's hungry work, making pencils all day long."

"They must be very long pencils," replied Mr. Vanderpuff, and the two shopkeepers shared a comfortable chuckle.

Between the queuing knees, Bridget glimpsed a slender, brown hand darting into the cabinet with gleaming, silver tongs. Then the brass till sang, the queue stepped eagerly forward, and beneath a tall chef's hat as bright and white as a whip of cream, appeared the great baker himself.

Mr. Ernest Vanderpuff.

Mr. Vanderpuff's Customers

behind the counter ✶ a spoiled dog ✶ new places

"Bridget!" cried Mr. Vanderpuff. "How did you sleep, my dear?"

The whole queue turned around and Bridget, for the first time in her whole life, blushed.

She turned to Pascal, who waved his hands frantically.

"None of them can see me!" he said. "Say something!"

"I... um..." Bridget stammered. She had never been asked such a thing before—Miss Acrid didn't care in the least how her Errant Childs slept. "Sleepily? And then, when I woke up, my covers did the *strangest*—"

"We'll talk about that in a moment," said Mr. Vanderpuff quickly, lifting a golden chain at the side of the counter. "Come, sit beside me while I serve these lovely people."

"What a sweet child," said a lady carrying a tiny dog in a handbag.

"What incredible hair," said a man covered in daubs of paint.

"What a nice queue," said Bridget, ducking under the chain.

Everyone laughed, then muttered happily to each other as they shuffled forward.

"Here you are," said Mr. Vanderpuff, brushing flour from a rickety stool. "This is the end of the morning rush. Once everyone has their cakes and bakes, I'll close the shop and we can have a little chat."

"All right," said Bridget, hopping onto the stool.

"Now," said Pascal. "*Watch.*"

Bridget was not, naturally, a patient girl. Her mind was constantly hopping from thing to thing like a frog on a boiling pond. Normally, the prospect of waiting for a long queue of people to be served would have driven her to the magnifying glass secreted in her hair and her bracelet of nano-novels.

But Vanderpuff's Bake Shop was not a normal place—it was, in fact, the least normal place she'd ever been.

She was sitting *behind* the counter of the world's most beautiful bake shop, waiting to speak to her new guardian, the man who had freed her from the Orphanage for Errant Childs after a lifetime of being screamed at by Miss Acrid.

"Are you all right?" asked Pascal.

And she had a new, invisible elf friend sitting on her shoulder.

"Yes," she whispered, without moving her lips.[24] "I just love it so much."

---

[24] Bridget had mastered ventriloquy during a spare half hour in Miss Acrid's dungeon.

Bridget could see on the faces of the villagers as they paid for their cakes how jealous they were of her being so close to Mr. Vanderpuff—how dearly they would love to be on the shop side of the counter.

And it *was* like being invited into a great secret. The counter, which was glass and shiny and grand on the customer side, was more functionally scruffy from behind.

But, Bridget thought, just as glorious.

She could feel the heat of the lights that beamed down on the pastries and cakes. She could see the clasps and handles with which Mr. Vanderpuff slid open the glass doors. There were shelves underneath for the boxes and bags, a hook for the tongs, a broom, a dustpan, and a pair of clogs she realized must be Mr. Vanderpuff's—who was moving over the floorboards in his bare feet.

She felt very important and special indeed.

"Good morning, Ms. French," he said, clapping his hands. "And how is little Henri?"

The dog—which Bridget could see had the strangulated, bug-eyed expression of tiny, spoiled dogs everywhere—barked twice, then growled.

"He has a touch of the collywobbles, Mr. Vanderpuff," said Ms. French, primping the side of her towering Afro. "I thought I'd get him an *extra* Splendiferous Pastrycase to cheer him up."

"Five Splendiferous Pastrycases, then?"

"He does love them so," said Ms. French, moving Henri's little paw so it looked like he was waving.

"Woof!" Henri barked.

"Splendid," chuckled Ms. French, as Mr. Vanderpuff lifted five golden pastries into a bag.

She tottered off, and the paint-spattered man stepped up.

"A Butterunctious Crunch, please, Mr. Vanderpuff," he said, tucking a thin paintbrush behind his ear.

"Of course, Mr. Pringle," said Mr. Vanderpuff, lifting a bronzed cube of lavishly decorated cake into a box with his tongs. "And how is Mrs. Pringle?"

"Quite well, thank you," said the painter, secreting the Butterunctious Crunch somewhere in his spattered overall. "Thinks she'll finish her masterpiece this afternoon, in fact. *Moonlight Sunshine*, she calls it. This is a treat for when she's done."

"Lovely," said Mr. Vanderpuff. "I look forward to the exhibition."

Mr. Pringle laughed.

"Oh," he said, shaking his head with a fond, faraway expression, "she won't be *showing* it to anyone, old boy. As soon as she's finished, she'll set the whole thing on fire and start a new one. Same as last time."

Mr. Vanderpuff laughed and turned to the final customer—a tall lady with neatly pinned hair and a shiny chain around her neck.

"And what can I get for you, ma'am?"

"My usual, please, Mr. Vanderpuff—all the Vanderpuff Deelites you've got left," said the lady, smiling at Bridget.

The Deelite was a tower of crisp, buttery-looking pastry, with layers of white cream and bright, red jam among the spots of strawberry. Mr. Vanderpuff lifted the last two into a box.

"How are things in the halls of power?" he asked, adding with a whisper to Bridget, "This is the mayor of Belle-on-Sea!"

Even very important people buy cakes here! thought Bridget, who had never seen a mayor before.

"Everything is wonderful, thank you," said the mayor. "We're all ready for this weekend's Wintersmith Fete, right here in Candlewick Place. There'll be games, singing—and the Wintersmith himself will be there to hand out presents to the children! You're making your usual contribution, I hope?"

"If I'm still invited, ma'am," said Mr. Vanderpuff.

The mayor threw back her head and laughed.

"Why, your cakes are the very centerpiece of the whole event! What are you making this year?"

Mr. Vanderpuff blushed a little.

"I haven't decided yet, ma'am," he said.

"Well, I'm sure it'll be simply *delicious*," said the mayor, tapping her bony nose. "And who is this hiding under all that hair?"

Bridget stood up and curtsied awkwardly.

"Bridget Baxter, ma'am," she said.

"Pish posh with all that curtsying," replied the mayor. She put out her hand. Bridget shook it. "You've come to live with Mr. Vanderpuff?"

"Yes, ma'am."

"Capital! He's a very fine man and you'll be very happy here—there are lots of children on Candlewick Place. Did you know that Belle-on-Sea is built on an old silver mine? Or that we've won the Handsomest Hamlet award seven years in a row?"

"No, ma'am."

"Well, it's true! What's your favorite Vanderpuff bake?"

"I don't know," said Bridget. "I only ate a baked thing for the first time yesterday, and Mrs. Pobydd made that one."

"And Mrs. Pobydd is . . . ?"

"The cook. In the Orphanage."

"I *see*," said the mayor, with a sympathetic tilt of her head. "An Errant Child."

Pascal put his hand on the top of Bridget's ear.

"Yes, ma'am," she said.

The mayor gave Bridget a wide, happy grin.

"Not anymore, hey!" she said. "Look after this girl, Mr. Vanderpuff — I have a feeling she'll be keeping you on your toes!"

Mr. Vanderpuff gave Bridget a wink.

"I hope so, ma'am," he said.

The bell chimed as the mayor stepped out onto Candlewick Place, clutching her cake box close to her chest.

"They all seemed so happy," said Bridget.

Mr. Vanderpuff nodded.

"That's why people come here," he said, "to feel happy. This is not any old baker's shop — it is, if I may say so myself, the finest bakery in the whole world."

"He's right," said Pascal. "It is!"

Mr. Vanderpuff spun the *CLOSED* sign and pulled down the blind.

"Come on," he said, clapping his hands with a puff of flour, "I'll give you the grand tour!"

12

The Grand Tour

cakes ✳ invisible magic ✳ a warning

"Let's start in the shop," said Mr. Vanderpuff. "Look in the display cabinet. What do you see?"

"Cakes," said Bridget. "And pastries."

"Very good. Here."

Mr. Vanderpuff dropped a strawberry onto Bridget's palm. Bridget ate the strawberry. It was very cold and very sweet.

"This is what's left after a busy morning," said Mr. Vanderpuff. "On this shelf, Splendiferous Pastrycases and Butterunctious Crunches. Below that, my much-loved Caramagnificent Donuts and Fabananananana Swirls.[25] And here is where I display my most special and prized creation—the Vanderpuff Deelite. The mayor, as you know, bought the last two. Now, look again."

Bridget leaned forward. She ran her eyes over the trays of treats.

There were cakes. And there were pastries.

She felt a creep of embarrassment—which turned quickly to panic.

What is Mr. Vanderpuff expecting me to say— and what will happen if I can't say it? Will I have failed some sort of test? Will Mr. Vanderpuff send me back to the Orphanage?

"I still see cakes and pastries," she whispered. "Only now I know their names."

"Take your time," said Mr. Vanderpuff gently.

Bridget's hand went automatically to her hair— but as she rifled through the gadgets and tools, she realized there was no clever invention that could help her, no lock she could pick that would reveal this secret.

---

[25] These had first been called Fabananananananananana, then Fabanananananana, and then, finally, Fabananananana Swirls. Mr. Vanderpuff's problem hadn't been *how* to spell the word, so much as when to stop.

She just had to do as Mr. Vanderpuff said, and take her time. So, she did.

And something happened.

Instead of simply *seeing* rows of cakes, she *felt* the excited, bubbly joy of customers making their selection; the heart-skipping glee of people sharing their Crunches and Swirls with people they loved.

And as she looked at all the beautiful Vanderpuff creations, she felt that warm glow moving from the soles of her feet up through her tummy and into the ends of her hair.

It was the most amazing feeling Bridget had ever experienced in her life.

These were not simply *cakes*, they were *Vanderpuff's* cakes—and she could *see* the happiness and wonder and joy glowing around them.

"Goodness," she said.

Mr. Vanderpuff gave her a smile so wide it nearly touched his ears.

"So, you *do* see it!" he said, giving her a little nudge. "This is what we sell here, Bridget—not simply pastries and cakes, but excitement and *love*. And *that's* what makes this the finest baker's shop in the world!"

Bridget nodded.

"It's like invisible magic," she said. "This is a magical place."

"It's a magical place," agreed Mr. Vanderpuff.

"It really is," said Pascal.

Mr. Vanderpuff glanced at the elf on Bridget's shoulder, then frowned.

"Thought I heard something there," he said, smiling.

"Told you," sighed Pascal.

Bridget patted his knee as Mr. Vanderpuff pulled the tassel on a lamp.

A panel in the wall slid aside.

"A secret passageway!" cried Bridget, clapping her hands. "I love secret passageways!"

"There are lots more," said Mr. Vanderpuff. "I dare say you'll have fun trying to find them."

"Oh, I will," said Bridget, running her hands over the other lamps. "I'm good at

that sort of thing."[26]

Mr. Vanderpuff laughed.

"I bet you are," he said, tousling her hair. "Come on."

They climbed a rickety wooden staircase and emerged from behind the grandfather clock outside Bridget's bedroom.

"Aha!" cried Bridget, glancing at Pascal. "I *knew* there was something about that clock. This is how I shall come downstairs from now on."

"A grand idea," said Mr. Vanderpuff. "Now—"

"Why's there a missing painting?" asked Bridget.

Mr. Vanderpuff froze.

"How do you know there's one missing?" he said softly.

"You can see the shadow where the dust landed around it," said Bridget. "And here, look—a bit of gold paint from the frame, which was up-and-down shaped."

"Oh, you are nosey, aren't you?" breathed Pascal.

---

[26] The Errant Childs had always come to Bridget to help find their lost toys and trinkets. In her recovery of missing hairpins and teddy bears around the Orphanage and its grounds, she had also found three treasure chests, nine dinosaur bones, seven crop circles and one ghost.

Mr. Vanderpuff had gone slightly pale.

"Up-and-down shaped?" he said.

"Yeah," said Bridget, nodding and making a box shape with her hands. "When it's a picture of a hill or something, it's like a rectangle on its side. This is like a rectangle standing up, so it's probably a picture of a person."

"A portrait," whispered Mr. Vanderpuff.

"That's it!" said Bridget, clicking her fingers. "It was a portrait of someone. Why's it missing?"

"It was a picture of Etta, my wife," said Mr. Vanderpuff.

A strange look came into his eyes, as though he was seeing something that was both right in front of him and somehow very far away.

"When she died, I took the picture down and locked it away."

"Why?" asked Bridget.

Mr. Vanderpuff touched the empty space on the wall.

"Because it hurt my heart so to see it there, knowing she wouldn't be waiting for me. And then, when I finally felt ready to have it back, when I *needed* to see her . . . I had lost the key."

"The Locked and Secret Door," Bridget whispered. "That's where Mrs. Vanderpuff's painting is!"

Pascal nodded silently.

"She used to sing to me," he said, "while Mr. V was inventing his fabulous bakes. She'd sing, and her voice would carry through the whole bakery."

The clock ticked beside them. Bridget looked at her shoes.

They still had some dungeon dirt on the toes.

Etta spoke to Mr. Vanderpuff in his dream, she thought, *it's because of her he came to find me — it's because of her that I'm here, and not in the Orphanage.*

"I'm good at finding things," she said. "Maybe I could help?"

Mr. Vanderpuff shook his head as though waking himself up.

"Thank you, my dear," he said, refocusing on Bridget's face, "but I fear that door is closed to me forever. Now," he added, gesturing to Bridget's Room of Bed, "you wanted to talk about *this*."

The Sentient Covers gave Bridget a ripple of welcome.

"Hello!" said Bridget, waving back.

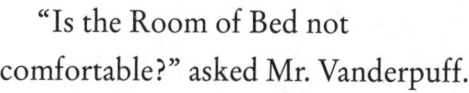

"Is the Room of Bed not comfortable?" asked Mr. Vanderpuff.

"Oh, no, it's incredibly comfortable." Bridget remembered the upside-down starfish shape the covers had spun her into. "It's the most comfortable I've ever been."

"She nearly couldn't get up at all!" said Pascal, hopping onto her head and addressing Mr. Vanderpuff directly.

Mr. Vanderpuff twiddled a finger in his ear, then pressed his hand to his chest.

"What a tremendous relief," he said. "Those covers are extremely special. That was why I shushed you in the shop—we can't have any of the villagers knowing we have one."

"Why not?"

"*Everyone* wants a set for their own bed! There would be pandemonium in the streets! A siege of the bake shop!"

"So how did you manage to get one?"

Mr. Vanderpuff tapped his nose.

"Mrs. MacGlover, who makes them, has a weakness for Fabananana Swirls."

"I see," said Bridget. "Is Mrs. MacGlover a witch?"

The covers rippled.

Mr. Vanderpuff gave Bridget a serious look.

"Yes," he said, after a moment. "But that's a very big secret. Do you understand?"

"Of course," said Bridget, who felt very excited about sleeping in a witchy bed.[27]

"Is there anything else you need?" asked Mr. Vanderpuff.

"What do you mean?"

"For your bedroom. Perhaps . . . what do little girls like? Slippers, or . . . a hairbrush?"

"Oh, my hair eats hairbrushes," said Bridget. "One time, Miss Acrid tried to straighten it as a punishment for painting the pigs purple, and my fringe had a three-course meal: a bristle brush for starters, a detangler for main, and a comb for dessert. It even burped."

"Yes, you mentioned that before," said Mr. Vanderpuff, shuddering.

Pascal chuckled.

"He *hates* burps—*and* farts," he said. "Even when he's on his own, he has to leave the room."

---

[27] Bridget's own witchy ancestor, Bridgette, had slept in a hammock spun from palm fronds and grass.

"Sorry," said Bridget, remembering the way Mr. Vanderpuff had reacted to Miss Acrid's fishy burp.

"That's all right, my dear," said Mr. Vanderpuff. "I had some chef's whites made for you. I hope you don't mind."

He reached into the room, pulled a drawer out of the wall, then handed her a pile of neatly folded linen.

"Thank you," said Bridget, who had never worn anything other than an Orphanage uniform.

"You're most welcome, my dear!" said Mr. Vanderpuff, hopping onto the banister and sliding down, his apron flapping behind him like a flag. "Now, come on!"

Bridget and Pascal slid after him, and together they sped back to the ground floor.

"This," said Mr. Vanderpuff, straightening his white hat, "is the Locked and Secret Door. The door I was telling you about—for which I've lost the key. Nobody can get it open, and nothing can get through. It's quite hopeless."

He laid his palm flat against the door's surface, as though he could feel his wife's picture on the other side.

Bridget looked at the heavy wood, iron hinges and iron locks. Every hair on the back of her neck was standing to attention with the desire to make the Locked and Secret Door *un*locked and *un*secret as soon as possible.

Before so much as a day had passed in the home of Mr. Vanderpuff, she had experienced life-changing friendship and kindness.

She thought of herself in the Orphanage for Errant Childs—and touched the empty thumb where Tom's ring had sat.

"I'll get it open for you, Mr. Vanderpuff," she said, her lips thin and determined. "I promise I will."

"It's a lovely thought, my dear." Mr. Vanderpuff smiled ruefully, then tapped the tip of her nose. "We shall start your daily lessons at ten o'clock, but first," he clapped his hands, "breakfast!"

13

Breakfast

croissants ✳ invisible bananas ✳ exploding tastebuds

"These are splendid," said Bridget, smoothing the front of her chef's whites. "Thank you." She sat on a chair in the apartment's kitchenette, then crossed her ankles.

"You're quite welcome," said Mr. Vanderpuff, pouring dark, velvety coffee. "To bake in my bakery, you must *dress* like a baker!"

"You look super," said Pascal. "Why, you could pass for a Butters!"

Having spent every single day of her nine years in an Orphanage uniform, Bridget felt very glad to have new

clothes—but strange without her secret pockets.

She'd hidden as much as she could in her hair, and placed the rest in her Sentient Covers, which had wrapped them up tightly.

A lifetime of Miss Acrid's confiscations made her incapable of leaving her things lying around.

"Now that you're dressed like a baker," said Mr. Vanderpuff, "we can begin our day together."

"In the bakery?"

"Not yet," said Mr. Vanderpuff. "There's one thing a baker *always* does before baking—eat a tasty breakfast!"

He handed her a perfect pink box, tied with a vivid green ribbon, bearing on its sides, in golden letters, the word:

Bridget's eyes widened. The box was an immaculate cube, its edges sharp and smooth, and its pink surface almost iridescent in the snow-light. Touching it seemed somehow impossible, as though it might burst under her touch, like a perfect, shimmering bubble.

But she wanted what was inside very much indeed.

With another glance at Mr. Vanderpuff, she took the ribbon between her thumb and forefinger—and pulled.

The box fell open like the petals of a blooming flower, so suddenly it seemed to vanish.

Bridget held on to the ribbon.

"These are what Tom and I ate yesterday," she said, looking at the bronzed, flaky pastries.

"Who's Tom?" asked Mr. Vanderpuff.

"He is . . . he *was* my best friend," said Bridget. She touched the place where the ring had sat. "In the Orphanage."

Mr. Vanderpuff nodded.

"It's hard to lose someone," he said.

Bridget looked up.

"Like you lost Etta?"

"Yes. And one of the things that helps me . . . feel . . . all my feelings about her, is thinking about the moments we shared. So, perhaps you can think about your friend as you eat, and I shall think about my wife. But first, I have a question about these croissants."

"Oh good," said Bridget, "I love questions."

"I thought you might," chuckled Mr. Vanderpuff.

"Is that how you say it?" asked Bridget. "Croissant? Tom and I thought they were called *kwassongs*."

"A crrroissant," said Mr. Vanderpuff, rolling the *r* sound around his mouth. "And my question is this: why are there *two* croissants in your box?"

Bridget felt her brain kick into motion. *Maybe it's a tradition,* she thought, *or . . . croissants come in pairs . . . like turtledoves, or trousers.*

She glanced up at Mr. Vanderpuff, who was sipping his coffee and watching her keenly.

Maybe it's symbolic, she thought, *the way a red rose*

is symbolic of love . . . two croissants are symbolic of . . . breakfast?

She looked at Pascal, who winked.

And then she realized.

Two croissants weren't traditional, and they weren't symbolic. The answer was much more simple—and much more important—than that.

"There's two croissants because there's two of us," she said. "We're going to eat them together."

"*Exactly*, my dear," said Mr. Vanderpuff, lifting his croissant from the box.

"Well done!" said Pascal, happy tears forming in his eyes. "I think you're going to fit right in here, oh yes."

Mr. Vanderpuff tore the croissant in two, sending a flurry of flakes onto the table.

"Croissants are made by folding butter into dough," he said, "lots and lots of butter, in fact, over and over again. They are my absolute favorite bake to eat. They were Etta's favorite, too."

Bridget picked up her croissant. It was still warm, and smelled very buttery indeed. Her tummy started dancing in anticipation.

"Now, my dear, before we even begin your

lessons—before we crack a single egg—I want you to understand my first and most important principle: baking is best when it is *shared*. Everything in life, whether you're climbing a hill or singing a song, is far more pleasurable when shared with someone you love. The greatest joy I get from baking doesn't come from the invention of a new type of cream bun, or the reputation my shop has in the village— my greatest joy comes from the excitement in my customers' faces. I think you saw it this morning."

"I did," said Bridget. "It was wonderful."

"I think so, too. Now," Mr. Vanderpuff sat forward and smiled, creasing the corners of his eyes, "some people put chocolate on their croissants, some smother them in jam. I prefer simply to tear a little piece off and dip it in my coffee, as they do in France."

Bridget's eyes widened.

"You've been to *France*?" she breathed.

"Etta and I baked our way around the world," said Mr. Vanderpuff. "We made lots of friends."

He dipped the piece of croissant in his cup, and closed his eyes with satisfaction as he chewed.

"Should I do that with my glass of milk?" asked Bridget.

"You may enjoy your croissant however you wish."

Bridget thought back to the bowls of cold slop the Childs were given for breakfast in the Orphanage.

"Might I try some jam?" she asked.

"Right over there," said Mr. Vanderpuff, pointing to a cabinet on the wall. "We have quite a few different kinds."

"What kinds are they?"

Mr. Vanderpuff puffed out his cheeks.

"Oh, there's apple, *cran*apple, berry, *cran*berry, apricot, plum, courgette, cherry, *black* cherry, *gummi* cherry, damson, cantaloupe, cardamom, carrot, chili, spicy chili, *super* spicy chili, invisible, banana, *invisible* banana, rhubarb, mango, peach, pear, pomegranate; and, of course, your berry basics: strawberry, raspberry, gooseberry, blueberry, cloudberry, candleberry, glowberry, blackberry and buckthorn. I also make orange and tangerine marmalades; lemon, lime and kumquat curds, *and* there's some happy heather honey from my own hives."

"Goodness," said Bridget, who had only ever seen jam once, on Miss Acrid's table on the other side of the Orphanage canteen. "I thought the only flavor it came in was 'red.'"

She regarded the cupboard. It was a small box—wooden, like the rest of the kitchen, and painted a pale, herby green.

I don't see how this tiny thing could hold so many flavors, she thought, opening the latch.

The cupboard doors swung open, releasing a series of soaring shelves that unfolded like an octopus stretching its legs; a spiderwork of concertina brass which sprung out so quickly that in a matter of seconds the tiny box had grown tenfold to tower over her, its rickety shelves filled with columns of gleaming, labeled jars.

"Help yourself," said Mr. Vanderpuff.

"I should have known it would be something incredible," said Bridget. "*Everything* here is incredible!"

She ran her finger along the labels.

There was the chili, and the damson, and the

candleberry[28] . . . the citrus curds and the marmalades, and—a gap.

"Why is this space empty?"

Mr. Vanderpuff glanced up.

"It's not," he said, "that's the invisible banana jam."

"*Invisible banana?*"

"Well, I *call* it 'invisible banana jam' but, of course, that's not *really* what it is."

"Oh," said Bridget. "What is it, then?"

Mr. Vanderpuff took another sip of coffee.

"It's more of a jelly," he said.

Bridget turned back to the expanding jam cupboard and lifted herself on tiptoe. "Can I try the strawberry, please?"

"Of course, my dear. Start with a classic!" said Mr. Vanderpuff.

He reached over and lifted down a square jar full of bright red jam. It had a checked gingham lid and a label written in scratchy green pen. "Here you go. Spoon some onto your plate, then dip in a piece of croissant. I think you'll find it most delicious."

---

[28] Delicious, but the wicks *do* get stuck in your teeth.

Mr. Vanderpuff's strawberry jam seemed to glow in the light from the little window, as though the morning sun was dancing through the strawberries that speckled the jar like buried jewels. Bridget spooned some onto her plate. Its smell was clean and sweet, and it was much runnier than she'd been expecting—the jam she'd seen Miss Acrid eating had been cut into slices.

She tore off a piece of her croissant. The dough inside was very stretchy, and yellow with butter. She breathed in its scrumptious aroma.

"*Beautiful*," said Pascal. "He really does make wonderful croissants."

"It is beautiful, isn't it?" said Bridget, too loudly. "Almost too beautiful to eat."

"Nothing is too beautiful to eat," said Mr. Vanderpuff. "On you go!"

"All right," said Bridget. She dipped the croissant into her bright puddle of jam, closed her eyes—and popped it in her mouth.

She knew it would be tasty . . . but nothing could have prepared her for just *how* tasty, *how* delicious, *how* exciting and

how fabulous it really was.

Her heart fizzed as though struck by lightning, and her tastebuds exploded like fireworks. Never before, even when she'd shared Mrs. Pobydd's bake with Tom, had she tasted anything like the soft dough's buttery warmth or the flaky pastry's bitter bite—and beside and on top and all around those flavors swirled the cool, sweet jam—so sharp and red with strawberry goodness she might have been biting the fruit straight from the plant.

"What do you think, my dear?" asked Mr. Vanderpuff.

Bridget opened her eyes. Her heart was pounding. She popped the rest of the croissant and jam into her mouth, holding on to the edge of the table to stop herself from fainting with the sheer, overwhelming rush of deliciousness.

She swallowed.

"I think I'm ready for my first lesson," she said.

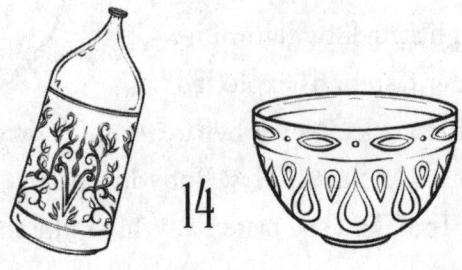

14

Lesson One

the giant mixing table ✳ cracking eggs ✳ disaster

Bridget climbed onto the stepladder at ten o'clock on the button.

The bakery had an expectant air, as though it were used to great things happening within its walls. Bridget stood beside Mr. Vanderpuff at the giant mixing table.

"Now, my dear," said Mr. Vanderpuff, as Pascal hopped, unnoticed, onto his shoulder, "what do you know about baking?"

"I know it's how you make croissants," said Bridget. "And cakes. And bread."

"Very good. Anything else?"

Bridget thought hard.

Arranged in front of her were bowls of many different sizes, a dozen enameled jugs, towers of egg boxes the color of plant pots, and a forest of wooden spoons. And there were other objects — things she'd never seen in her life — wiry round balls with handles, long flat sticks, silver-nozzled bags of see-though paper.

"I don't know," she said. "I only tried a baked thing for the first time yesterday morning."

"Yes, I heard you telling the mayor. Didn't you get cake on your birthday?"

"No, all the Childs had an Errant birthday."

"What do you mean?"

"Well..." Bridget, who'd read about birthday parties, and knew that other children woke up on their birthday feeling special and excited, looked at her shoes. "I don't know when my *real* birthday is. None of us did. We were all told our birthday was the first of June, and that's when we got our potato."

Mr. Vanderpuff went pale.

"Your *potato*?"

"Yes. We didn't get birthday cake — we got a raw

potato that we had to cook ourselves."[29]

Pascal's mouth fell open.

"Villainy!" he cried.

"I see," said Mr. Vanderpuff, and his lips went very thin. "Well, in that case I'm even more glad you're here, and not at that wretched place."

"Mrs. Pobydd, the Orphanage cook, baked all the time," said Bridget, feeling embarrassed. "But she was only allowed to bake for Miss Acrid, or for the Families who came once a year. And Miss Acrid never shared her bakes. She never shared anything."

"Then she has broken my first and most important principle. Do you remember it, my dear?"

"Baking is best when it's shared," said Bridget.

"Very good. But wait a moment—if Miss Acrid never shared her bakes, then how did you manage to try a croissant yesterday?"

Bridget fidgeted with her apron.

"I . . . borrowed it," she said.

"Borrowed?" said Mr. Vanderpuff, eyes twinkling.

---

[29] A gifted woodschild, Bridget was usually responsible for building the campfire on which the Errant Childs would bake their same-birthday potatoes.

"You mean you're going to give it back?"

Bridget met his unblinking gaze.

"Absolutely."

Mr. Vanderpuff laughed.

"Well, Miss Acrid is gone, and now you are in *our* bakery. Here is where you will learn to bake as I bake, to make croissants and loaves and every fabulous cake you have seen this morning and more besides. And to start any bake, we mix!"

"Wonderful!" cried Bridget, clapping her hands. She looked around the giant mixing table. "So . . . we stir things in a bowl?"

"There's a *little* more to it than that," giggled Pascal, resting his elbow on Mr. Vanderpuff's hat.

"You're partly right," said Mr. Vanderpuff. "But we don't just *stir* our ingredients, we beat, blend, cream, cut, fold, knead, sift and whip them. Watch . . ."

He threw two eggs in the air and cracked them as they fell.

Crack!
Crack!

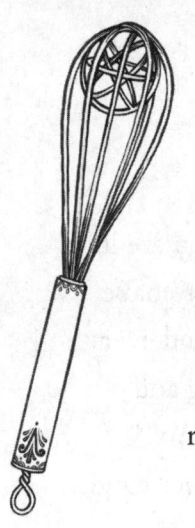

Two perfect eggs sat in a white bowl, their bright yolks watching Bridget like big bobbly eyes.

Bridget gasped. She'd hardly seen Mr. Vanderpuff's hands move. "Wow," she whispered.

"He's the best there is," said Pascal.

Mr. Vanderpuff lifted one of the wiry round things and held it to the light.

"Do you know what this is?"

"Umm..." said Bridget.

I'm used to knowing things! she thought. *Why don't I know this?*

"This," said Mr. Vanderpuff, "is a balloon whisk."

"Balloon whisk," said Bridget, filing the words away in her memory, as though placing a treasured object in a drawer.

"And we use this to *beat* our eggs. Like so..."

Mr. Vanderpuff thrust the whisk into the bowl and spun the eggs into a whirling blur. He tilted the bowl toward her, so she could see. The yolks had vanished, and were replaced by a pale-yellow liquid, which foamed with tiny bubbles.

"Beaten eggs," said Bridget. "Got it."

"Now, you try. Take an egg in your hand . . ."

Bridget lifted an egg.

". . . hold it so your thumb is along one side . . ."

Bridget moved her thumb along the side of the egg.

". . . and crack it gently on the side of the bowl," finished Mr. Vanderpuff, gently cracking his egg.

Bridget smashed her egg down, splintering the delicate shell and sending a big gloopy blob onto the table.

"Good grief!" said Pascal, wiping egg white from his eyebrows. "You're not using it to hammer in nails!"

"Oh, no!" cried Bridget. "I'm so sorry, I didn't mean to—"

"It's all *right*, my dear," chuckled Mr. Vanderpuff. "In fact, we're probably starting with the trickiest bit

of all. Eggs are delicate things—sometimes even I have to fish a little piece of shell from my bowl!"[30]

"Really?" asked Bridget.

"Absolutely," said Mr. Vanderpuff.

Bridget picked up another egg and tried to crack it as *gently* as she could.

"Good heavens," said Mr. Vanderpuff, staring at the orangey splat on the ceiling. "I've never seen *that* happen before."

"I can't do it!" said Bridget, throwing up her hands. "I've never not been able to do something before!"

Then she thought of the Locked and Secret Door, and its unpickable lock.

What if I can't do anything outside the Orphanage? she thought. Then a horrible idea formed in her mind.

What if losing Tom's ring has put a curse on me?

Mr. Vanderpuff dabbed her nose with flour.

"Baking is complicated," he said calmly. "It takes people *years* to master. Some people *never*

---

[30] Using another piece of shell, of course.

master it—that's why when a person makes excellent chocolate cake, or Wintersmith pudding, or dumplings, they become so well known and loved for it. Such things are very difficult."

"But there's instructions," said Bridget glumly, pointing at the recipe books on the shelf. "I can follow *instructions*—you just read what they say, and then do it."

Mr. Vanderpuff smiled.

"Here." He cracked another couple of eggs into a new bowl. "I'll crack them, and you whisk. How about that?"

Bridget felt a fist begin to squeeze her tummy. Of all the things she'd tried in her life, of all the challenges she'd ever faced, why did *baking*—the craft of her new guardian—have to be the *one* thing she couldn't do?

I must get this right, she thought. *If I can't bake properly, Mr. Vanderpuff might not let me stay. I'll have to go back to the Orphanage and Miss Acrid. And all this—Mr. Vanderpuff and the bake shop and Pascal—will be gone forever.*

She closed her eyes and spun the whisk. The metal loops clattered

and rang against the bowl, and Bridget concentrated as hard as she possibly could on moving her whisking arm in a tight circle, the way Mr. Vanderpuff had done.

I've got it this time! she thought. *I've done it!*

She stopped and opened her eyes.

Mr. Vanderpuff had taken off his glasses and was wiping them free of egg with a checkered cloth.

"Let's try kneading some dough instead," he said.

But before he could clear the mixing table, Bridget had leaped from her little steps and dashed from the bakery.

"Bridget!" shouted Pascal, running after her as fast as his tiny legs could carry him.

Bridget sped up the secret passageway and into her Room of Bed, where she threw on her old Orphanage uniform and climbed, face bright with embarrassment and shame, out the window.

15
Rooftopper

bird's-eye view ✷ Bridget's spectacular catch ✷
the wonder of failure

Bridget's nose filled with smells as she climbed the chimney stack. Alongside Vanderpuff's sweetness floated the stationer's light pencil wood, the florist's rich bloom, and the pet shop's animal warmth. She imagined the people working and laughing in their handsome shops—assisted, invisibly, by their elves.

Happy people, who were exactly where they were supposed to be.

"Oh, Tom," she said aloud. "I've ruined everything. Mr. Vanderpuff wants me to be a baker, and I can't even crack an egg!"

Belle-on-Sea gleamed below her, its cobbled streets busy with families stamping the snow from their boots and hugging their rosy-cheeked friends. Bridget gazed out through the jostle of ornate chimneys. The old mine's train track ran through the square, its bright bars of silver pointing to the distant speck of the Orphanage for Errant Childs.

Pascal fell out the attic window, wheezed dramatically, then climbed onto her knee.

"Whatever's the matter?" he said, once his breath had returned.

"It's no use," said Bridget. "I can't do it."

"Come now—"

"I *can't*! You saw me—I'm rubbish! I'm worse than rubbish!"

"Well, I don't think so," said Mr. Vanderpuff, climbing out from a hatch in the roof. He shivered. "Who are you talking to?"

Bridget met Pascal's eyes.

The elf shrugged.

"Tom," said Bridget.

Mr. Vanderpuff nodded.

"I talk to Etta all the time. It helps, I find. My goodness, what a little rooftopper you are—you got up here so quickly!"

Bridget nodded sullenly.

"I'm *good* at climbing things," she said.

"You really *are* used to being able to do *everything*, aren't you?" said Mr. Vanderpuff. He perched uncertainly on the edge of the chimney stack. "Did you know that failure is an essential ingredient for success?"

"That doesn't make any sense," said Bridget with a sniff.

Mr. Vanderpuff laughed.

"It does! There isn't a single piece of music that

was composed on the spot, and all the best stories took several goes to get right. I am the finest baker in the world, but not one of my recipes worked first time."

Bridget half turned her head.

"Really?"

"Really," said Mr. Vanderpuff seriously. "You have to fail in order to succeed, my dear. How do you think people learn new languages? Do you think they just open their mouths and start talking in Dutch, or Mandarin, or Swahili?"

"Well, no," said Bridget reluctantly. "But I wasn't trying to compose music *or* learn a language—I was only trying to crack an egg. *One* measly egg! Maybe it's best if . . . if I go back to the Orphanage."

"No!" screamed Pascal, slapping his hands against his cheeks. "You can't go!"

"Goodness, no, my dear!" said Mr. Vanderpuff. "I don't ever, ever want you to go back to that place for any reason! It doesn't matter about the eggs! We've got lots of eggs! What's a little yolk on one's eyeball, anyway?"

Bridget felt a tear roll down her cheek. She wiped it away quickly.

"It does matter," she said. "You wanted a child who could bake with you. And I can't do it."

Mr. Vanderpuff put his head to one side.

"I see," he said. He put his hand on his heart. "I don't want you to do anything that makes you uncomfortable, or sad, or nervous. I just want you to be happy. I'm sorry I started the lessons so quickly—I was being thoughtless. It's only your first day!"

Bridget sniffed. A rickety truck puttered along Candlewick Place, passing a pair of horses clip-clopping on the cobbles. The air smelled of lavender and snow, and Bridget heard the distant chuckle of the fountain.

"I love it here," she said. "It's the most amazing place I've ever seen—even the fountain is wearing a crown!"

"That's the Handsomest Hamlet crown," said Mr. Vanderpuff, following her stare. "It was on the clocktower last year."

Bridget sighed.

"I don't want to let you down. I let Tom down, and I can't bear it."

Mr. Vanderpuff settled nervously beside her and took in the view.

"Why do you think you let him down?"

"Because he gave me his ring to keep forever. It was the only thing he had in the whole world. And I lost it the same day, and I think I . . . I think I've been cursed."

Mr. Vanderpuff frowned.

"Cursed?"

"Yes," said Bridget, as Pascal patted her knee. "I lost the ring, and now I can't do *anything*. It's like I'm being punished."

"I'm not sure I believe in curses," said Mr. Vanderpuff.

"Have you ever *been* cursed?"

"Well, no," Mr. Vanderpuff admitted. "When did you lose the ring?"

"Yesterday," said Bridget. "Tom went to a new house with a new family. And I never even had the chance to say goodbye."

She burst into tears.

Mr. Vanderpuff reached over and put his hand on Bridget's shoulder.

"You think it's still in the Orphanage?"

Bridget shrugged.

"Or on the road to the village. But who knows?

I was in Miss Acrid's office, on the roof, in the dungeon—"

"The *dunge*—" Mr. Vanderpuff began, then shook his head. "Never mind that, I'm sure Tom knows how much you love him. That's all that matters, in the end. And you won't ever let me down."

"So, you don't want me to go back to Miss Acrid?"

Mr. Vanderpuff pulled a face, as though he'd just heard an enormous burp.

"I will *never* want you to return there," he said.

"Even if I can't crack eggs?"

"My dear, even if you cover me in eggs, even if you decide you never want to bake again, even if you burn my bakery to the ground—I will *never* want you to go back to that place." He shivered. "Shall we go inside? I'm getting a little chilly."

Bridget wiped her nose on her sleeve.

"All right," she said.

"You *can't* go," said Pascal. "You belong here, Bridget—you *saw* me straight away, the first time I'd been seen in years! Who else but a true baker could see a bakery elf?"

Bridget gave him a smile, then turned to Mr. Vanderpuff.

"I'm sorry I made you come up here," she said.

"Not at all! I've never been on my roof before, which is silly, when you think of it. After all, it's *my* roof! Now, for our *next* lesson," said Mr. Vanderpuff, stepping backward, "I thought we could—"

His heel landed on a patch of ice and—arms flailing, feet flying, mouth wide in terror—he fell.

Pascal jumped up in panic.

"Mr. V!" he cried, turning to Bridget. "Do something!"

"I'm coming, Mr. Vanderpuff!" shouted Bridget, running to the edge and throwing herself into the air.

The great baker was plummeting toward the cobbles, his apron flapping in the wind, his trousers snapping against his legs. People on the street had seen him, and were covering their mouths in horror.

"*Aaaaaaaaargh!*" shrieked Mr. Vanderpuff, bug-eyed with terror.

"Take my hand!" called Bridget, stretching toward him.

"AAAAAAAAAAAAAAAAARRRRRRRGH!" wailed Mr. Vanderpuff.

"Almost . . . there!" cried Bridget.

"AAAAAAAAAAAAAAAAAAAAAAAAAAAAAAAAAAAAAAAAAAAAAARRRRRRGH!" screamed Mr. Vanderpuff.

Then, as the ground rushed closer, their fingertips touched, their hands clasped, and Bridget deployed her paraskirt with a *whump* that knocked a startled pigeon off its perch and threw a cloud of snow into the air.

They landed with a gentle *puff*.

Mr. Vanderpuff opened his eyes. He ran his palm over the pavement and sagged with relief.

"You saved me," he said.

Bridget pulled her hair back and nodded.

"Of course. I told you I was brave."

Mr. Vanderpuff looked up at the roof. Bridget followed his gaze, and saw Pascal perched on the guttering, clapping excitedly.

"You saved my life," said Mr. Vanderpuff.

Bridget shrugged coyly.

"It was nothing," she said, blushing as the villagers burst into applause.

Mr. Vanderpuff brushed himself down.

"My dear," he said. "Anyone who can take such incredible risk can *certainly* also wield a *whisk*." He held out his arm. "Shall we?"

"Yes," said Bridget, as they walked through the door into the bake shop. "Yes. Let's whisk it."

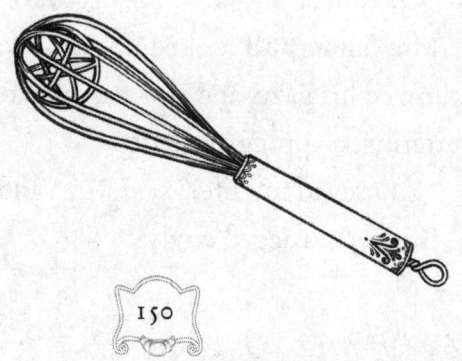

PART THREE
Bridget's Abominable Bakes

16
Scream Cream 1

"Let's put the eggs away," said Mr. Vanderpuff. "Instead, we're going to whip cream."

"All right," said Bridget, hopping on the spot like a boxer entering the ring.

"Do you remember what this is called?"

Bridget opened the drawer in her memory.

"A balloon whisk," she said.

"Well done!" said Pascal. "Don't worry—with a Butters by your side, you'll be a baking genius in no time!"

"Quite correct," said Mr. Vanderpuff. "This *golden* balloon whisk was a gift from my wife—I've made

all my most famous bakes with it. It's rather special—the little ball inside helps make billowing clouds of creamy loveliness."

"Billowing clouds," said Bridget, still hopping on the spot. "I can do this!"

"Everything should be nice and cold," said Pascal. "The bowl, the cream, the whisk—all of it must come straight from the refrigerator."

"Nice and cold," said Bridget, "got it."

Mr. Vanderpuff gave her a quizzical look.

"How did you know that?" he asked.

Bridget glanced at Pascal.

"I read it in a book," she said.

"Excellent!" replied the baker. "You're quite right—all of this equipment is nice and chilly."

Bridget and Pascal watched him pour cream into the mixing bowl. It fell in a glossy, shining ribbon, and smelled very good indeed.

"Some people use machines for this," said Mr. Vanderpuff with a haughty sniff. "But I like to do it the *proper* way."

He flicked the whisk from side to side with a soft chiming sound. After a moment, he swapped to his other hand, then kept going.

"It looks like hard work," said Bridget.

"It is, my dear. Nothing worth having is easily got."

The cream had begun to thicken—the whisk left traces behind it, like the wake of a ship. Mr. Vanderpuff, a sheen of perspiration forming on his brow, swapped hands again.

Bridget watched as the cream began to rise in the bowl, and listened as its movement became fluttery and thick.

"And there we have it," panted Mr. Vanderpuff, tilting the bowl toward her. "Whipped cream. Would you like to try some?"

Bridget took a spoonful.

"It's . . . nice," she said.

In truth, it was a little sour. Not what she'd been expecting at all.

"It needs to be sweetened!" chuckled Pascal. "Don't worry—it gets *very* delicious."

Mr. Vanderpuff smiled.

"I usually add a touch of cinnamon or vanilla to

make it lovely and sweet," he said.

"Could you add chocolate?" asked Bridget.

"Absolutely! We can try that once you've whipped yours. Here you go."

He handed Bridget a bowl and a jug of cream. She touched them. They were very cold.

"All right," she said, looking at Pascal, who winked.

"I believe in you!" he shouted.

Bridget poured the cream and stood over the bowl. The golden whisk was almost weightless in her hand.

Mr. Vanderpuff had flicked the whisk from side to side, not too fast, not too slow—filling the cream with air. It was hard work—but simple.

Simple, thought Bridget. *What could possibly go wrong?*

She started to whip.

At first, nothing happened.

Mr. Vanderpuff stood over her shoulder with Pascal

balanced invisibly on his shoulder, and they watched as the whisk clanged around.

It sounds all wrong, thought Bridget, panic rising in her chest. *Mr. Vanderpuff's whisk didn't* clang—*it* tinkled.

"Is this right?" she asked. "Am I doing it properly?"

"Sort of," said Mr. Vanderpuff, unable to disguise the worry in his voice. "Try moving the whisk in circles instead."

Bridget moved the whisk in circles. The clanging noise got worse.

Then something *very* strange happened.

17

Scream Cream 2

The cream, instead of growing light and fluffy, formed into a single blobby shape about the size of a cauliflower.

"Um, Mr. Vanderpuff?"

"Oh," said Mr. Vanderpuff. "Um . . . perhaps if you—"

The blob began to leap around the bowl.

"What's happening?" yelled Bridget, chasing it with the whisk.

"I have absolutely no idea!" shouted Pascal.

"I don't know, my dear!" said Mr. Vanderpuff. "I've never seen anything quite like it!"

The blob of cream gathered against the far side of the bowl, as

though poised for flight.

Then it *screamed*.

Bridget clapped her hands to her ears as the scream cream climbed from the bowl and dashed away, leaving splodgy white prints on the mixing table.

"Grab it!" shouted Mr. Vanderpuff, his own hands clamped to the sides of his head. "Don't let that cream get away!"

"I'll get it!" said Bridget, handing him the golden whisk and giving chase.

The noise was incredibly loud—it throbbed in her ears and shook her skeleton.

Pascal leaped away, his eyes screwed shut against its earsplitting shriek, then crashed into the window.

"Pascal!" cried Bridget.

"Make it *stop*!" cried Mr. Vanderpuff, falling to his knees in a cloud of flour.

Gritting her teeth, Bridget lifted a hand away from her head.

The cream's screams stabbed like a spear.

"Aaaargh!" she cried, rummaging

in her hair until she found two small pieces of cork—which she tucked snugly into her ears.

The noise muffled in an instant.

The cream's scream was still there, but only as a throbbing pulse—like music heard through a wall.

"All right, Cream!" she said, lifting a glass bowl from the shelf. "Time to get whipped!"

The cream—wobbling and screaming and splodging all over the place—darted into the sink.

With a twisting, balletic leap, Bridget spun through the air and trapped the cream safely under her bowl.

Mr. Vanderpuff eased his hands away from his ears, wafting the clouds of flour from his face.

"My goodness. I've never heard anything so noisy! You were only *whipping cream*! How did

you ... how did ... ?" He shook his head. "How did you make it do *that*?"

"I don't know," wheezed Bridget, flour settling on her hair as she piled recipe books on top of the glass bowl. "I tried to whip it, just like you showed me—I didn't mean to scare it!"

The cream strained against the glass, then, realizing it was safe from Bridget's whisk, curled up and went to sleep.

"Scream Cream," chuckled Mr. Vanderpuff, as Pascal clambered onto Bridget's shoulder. "Well, I never. Perhaps whipping things isn't your strong suit."

"Neither was cracking eggs," said the elf groggily, adding, when Bridget narrowed her eyes, "I'm sorry! I got a fright!"

"Well, then," said Mr. Vanderpuff. "I think that's enough for today. My ears are sore, and I need to reopen the shop."

"Does that mean our lessons are over?" asked Bridget.

"Certainly not," said Pascal.

"Not at all!" said Mr. Vanderpuff. "I just need to

get upstairs before the lunchtime customers arrive. We'll have another lesson tomorrow."

Bridget's heart skipped.

"I can try again?"

"Of course! Tomorrow, we'll try something *really* simple. Come on—to the bake shop!"

Bridget followed him out of the bakery, and felt, deep in her belly, a flicker of fear. This new life, with all its promise to fulfill her wildest dreams, still seemed impossible.

Mr. Vanderpuff was the nicest man in the whole world, but if she kept destroying everything, even he would eventually get cross enough to send her back to Miss Acrid.

No matter what he said.

Pascal patted the top of Bridget's head. "*Quite* a first try," he said, as Bridget ducked under the golden chain behind the counter.

"What a serious face," said Mr. Vanderpuff. "You must be having serious thoughts."

"I suppose I am," said Bridget. "I'm just so worried that losing Tom's ring really *has*—"

The bell over the door chimed, and the lunchtime customers filed in.

Bridget's Deelite

pastry * strawberries * cream

The rest of the day passed in a blur of smiling faces and buttery smells. When, finally, the shop closed, Bridget stumbled, exhausted, up the secret passageway toward her Room of Bed.

"Good night, Mr. Vanderpuff," she said. "Thank you for my lesson today. I'm sorry about all the screaming."

Mr. Vanderpuff stuck his head out from the kitchen.

"You're quite welcome, my dear—my ears have almost stopped ringing now. But come here a moment, before you turn in, would you?"

Bridget went into the kitchenette, and climbed onto her wobbly chair. The room smelled of coffee and bread, and the window over the hot tap had steamed up.

Pascal settled on her lap.

Mr. Vanderpuff knelt in front of her—then placed a small box in her hands.

"A little supper," he said. "To lift your spirits."

The box was another perfect pink cuboid, tied with another vivid green ribbon and bearing those magical golden letters.

"What's this?" asked Bridget.

Pascal's eyes widened.

"A Vanderpuff's Deelite, of course!"

"A Deelite? For me?"

"However did you know that?" asked Mr. Vanderpuff, with a funny smile.

"I can smell it," said Bridget. "All the strawberries."

"You're like a hound!" said Mr. Vanderpuff, tapping Bridget on the tip of her nose.

Bridget pulled the ribbon.

The box fell open.

"Oh, my," gasped Bridget. The aroma of strawberries and cream exploded like a great pink rocket, bursting in a shower of excitement that made her mouth salivate with anticipation.

She lifted the Deelite. It was surprisingly light, its pastry towers holding the rows of piped cream without bending or breaking.

This is a perfect thing, Bridget thought. *A perfect, perfect thing.*

She took a bite.

First, there was the crisp flake of pastry against her teeth and lips, and

the warmth of butteriness flooding her tongue in a cascade of bright, comforting yellows; then a swoop of cream, smooth as silken whispers, filling her with a glow that made her heart hum.

"*Mmmfffllmmm,*" Bridget managed to mumble before the lip-smacking sharpness of strawberries zinged through the cuddly cream cloud with a precision that had her gripping the table as though on the very edge of a delirious faint.

She finished the first mouthful. Then she had another, and another, and another, each as wondrous as the last.

And then it was finished, and Bridget looked up with eyes that shone with tears.

"I never knew food could taste so good," she said. "No, *good* is too small a word. That was incredible. Perfect. Completely perfect. Thank you, Mr. Vanderpuff. For everything you've done for me."

"It is my pleasure, my dear." Mr. Vanderpuff bowed. "Good night, then, Bridget. A final welcome to you, as we end our first day together in this house. Tomorrow, I hope you'll feel a little more settled, and a little more the day after that."

Bridget tied up her hair and gave him a shy smile.

She felt the bakery's old bones settling around her with a soft, satisfying creak. It was as though the whole building was giving her a hug.

"Good night, Mr. Vanderpuff," she said, rising and placing Pascal on her shoulder.

Mr. Vanderpuff watched her hands, apparently lifting an invisible object into the air.

"Good night, my dear," he said. "Sleep well."

Bridget paused in the hallway.

She could feel the Locked and Secret Door rumbling under her feet, like an engine buried in the ground.

She could feel its power over the bakery.

I'll pick that lock of yours soon, she thought, climbing into the Sentient Covers as Pascal settled between her feet. *And I'll get your painting back, Mr. Vanderpuff—you see if I don't.*

19

Suction Cupcakes 1

"You said whipping cream would be simple," said Bridget, as the clock struck ten.

She had slept wonderfully in the Sentient Covers, dreaming happily of Tom, until Pascal woke her up by tugging on her eyelids.

Mr. Vanderpuff had let her help with the morning rush, even allowing her to spin the paper bags in which he bundled the croissants. The villagers—including the teapotters,[31] Mrs. and Mrs. Yuen, and their daughter, Stacy—had smiled and laughed. It had been glorious.

---

[31] Yuens' Teapottery sold teapots in all shapes and sizes, their handles and spouts perfectly balanced for picking up and pouring out.

But now she was back in the bakery—the scene of yesterday's messy crime.

The Scream Cream was snoozing peacefully under the dome of the glass bowl, its snores echoing like the hum of a trapped bee. Bridget and Mr. Vanderpuff had tidied up as much of the chaos as they could, but the damage was still painfully obvious.

"I did say that," agreed Mr. Vanderpuff. "But cupcakes really *are* simple. And look—I've already made the cakes!"

He whipped back a cloth like a magician revealing his trick. A row of neat, round cakes sat in their tray, their tops shiny and round.

"Oh," said Bridget, trying to hide her disappointment. "So . . . what do *I* make? The cups?"

Mr. Vanderpuff laughed. From his perch on her shoulder, Pascal nudged Bridget's head.

"We make the *buttercream*," said the elf.

"Oh," said Bridget. "Buttercream."

"That's right!" said Mr. Vanderpuff. "Well done! And as every cake lover knows, that's the *best* bit of a cupcake."

Bridget rolled up her sleeves.

"All right," she said. "Let's do it."

"That's the spirit! We start by whisking the—"

"I'm not sure I should use the whisk," said Bridget, glancing at the sleeping Scream Cream.

Mr. Vanderpuff nodded slowly.

"She's got a point, boss," said Pascal.

"You're probably right," said Mr. Vanderpuff.

Bridget blinked.

There was no mistaking it that time—Mr. Vanderpuff *had* heard the elf speak.

He just didn't *realize* he'd heard him.

She looked at Pascal, who smiled excitedly.

"Well," said Mr. Vanderpuff, "*I'm* going to whisk this butter until it's extremely, wonderfully, gloriously soft . . . ! Now, we add the icing sugar. It's in the bowl by your elbow."

Bridget picked up a bowl of white powder.

"This?" She took a sniff. "It smells very sweet."

"Oh, it is—icing sugar is super, super sweet! And absolutely scrumdiddlyicious, of course! In it goes." Bridget tipped in the icing sugar. "And so does a teaspoon of vanilla and a pinch of salt."

Bridget made a face.

"Salt?"

"Oh, absolutely. We use lots of salt in baking.

Very important."

"Salt? In cakes?"

"Yes!"

"But . . . in the Orphanage, we put salt in our gruel. It goes in *cakes*?"

Mr. Vanderpuff laughed.

"Salt is one of the most important things in all cooking, my dear. Without it, the world would taste very bland indeed."

Bridget looked at Pascal.

The elf nodded.

"Just not *too* much," he said.

"All right," said Bridget, "I suppose you're the genius."

"Exactly," said Mr. Vanderpuff, giving the mixture another good whisk. He took a little taste of the buttercream and shuddered with happiness.

Bridget leaned over the bowl.

"Is it finished? Can I taste it?"

"In a moment, my dear. As you can see, it's still a little dry. What do you think we should add?"

Bridget thought.

"Water?"

"Milk," said Mr. Vanderpuff firmly. "Milk is the

baker's friend. We need just a few tablespoons."

He looked expectantly at Bridget.

"*Oh*," she said, straightening her chef's hat. "You want me to do it?"

"These are *your* cupcakes, my dear."

Bridget picked up the first thing within reach.

"Is this a tablespoon?"

"That's an oven glove," said Mr. Vanderpuff.

"Ha!" cried Pascal.

Bridget tried again.

"This?"

"Lemon zester."

"This?"

"Ice cream scoop."

"This?"

"Spatula."

"This?"

"Newspaper."

"This?"

"Masher. Peeler. Colander. Frying pan. My dear, it's a large *spoon*—don't overthink it!"

Bridget scanned the array of silverware.

"This?" she said, holding one up and closing her eyes.

"She's done it!" Pascal clapped, his face pink with delight. "I can't remember the last time I had this much fun!"

"That's it!" cried Mr. Vanderpuff. "We'll make a baker of you yet, Bridget Baxter—now that you know a spoon from an oven glove, there'll be no stopping you!"

Bridget's chef's hat fell over her eyes. She pushed it back and blew up a tendril of fringe.

"You're making fun of me," she said. "I can tell."

"A gentle tease, my dear," said Pascal and Mr. Vanderpuff together.

They looked at each other. Mr. Vanderpuff shook his head.

"Too much coffee again, Ernest," he muttered, then he looked at Bridget. "Now, come on—three tablespoons of milk. Just three. And we're done!"

Bridget gripped the tablespoon in her left hand. With her right, she lifted the glass bottle of milk.

Mr. Vanderpuff and Pascal watched with bated breath, neither of them blinking, their eyes fixed on the trembling spoon.

"Here goes," she said.

And tilted the bottle.

20

Suction Cupcakes 2

A huge glug of milk splashed into the bowl, knocking the spoon from her hand and throwing up the mixture in a great, sweet wave.

"Aaaaaargh!" yelled Bridget, thudding the milk bottle back onto the table. "I didn't mean it!"

"Look out!" yelled Mr. Vanderpuff, grabbing Bridget and Pascal and running for cover. "The mixture is loose!"

The buttercream sloshed all over the cakes Mr. Vanderpuff had made, smothering their shining tops with splodges of bright, gloopy icing.

The bowl spun on its edge, toppled over, then smashed on the floor.

Silence filled the bakery, quickly replaced by the

Scream Cream's buzzing snores.

Mr. Vanderpuff peered out from behind the fridge.

"You were only pouring *milk*," he said, a terrified awe creeping into his voice.

"And it looks like it worked!" Bridget cried in delight, leaping up and running over to the tray of cupcakes.

"Wait! We don't know if—" Mr. Vanderpuff began.

"It'll be fine! I'm just going to—"

Bridget slipped on a smudge of butter and flew high in the air.

"Bridget!" shouted Pascal, as Bridget landed, headfirst, on the tray of cupcakes.

The cupcakes shot upward as though fired from a cannon, spinning as they went and spraying milky buttercream all over the bakery, until . . .

SPLAT!

"Goodness," said Bridget, picking herself up and dragging the hair from her eyes.

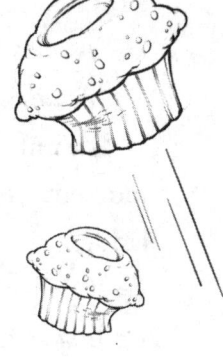

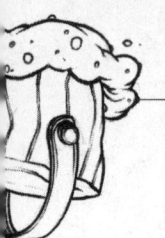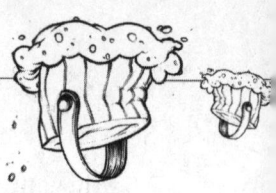

"Oh, dear," said Mr. Vanderpuff.

"How fabulous!" said Pascal, gazing up in wonder.

The cupcakes had stuck to the ceiling: stuck *completely*—as though coated in the world's stickiest Super Glue.

"How have you done *that*?" said Mr. Vanderpuff.

"Not to worry!" said Bridget, jumping onto the table and vaulting on top of the fridge. "I can get them down! I just need"—she rummaged in her hair, gripping and rejecting various hidden objects until—"this!"

She withdrew a short, wooden tube, and held it aloft.

"A telescope?" asked Mr. Vanderpuff.

"A *ladder*," said Bridget, rolling her eyes.

She unfolded the tube, spun it around, and in a moment, she was holding a long, sturdy-looking ladder.

"Oh, isn't that clever?" said Mr. Vanderpuff, smiling as he wiped milk from his forehead. "But I

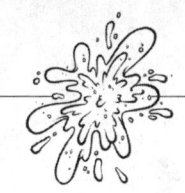

do worry that you'll hurt yourself."

Bridget raised an eyebrow.

"I leaped from the roof of the Orphanage for Errant Childs and landed in your car, didn't I?"

Mr. Vanderpuff smiled.

"I've never had such a fright. Until I fell off the roof, anyway."

"When I saved you!" said Bridget.

"Again, that is true," admitted Mr. Vanderpuff. "Although it's hard not to make a connection between my being terrified and your arrival."

"Pure coincidence," said Bridget. "I think I can shift a few cupcakes from the ceiling, don't you?"

"If anyone can," said Pascal, grinning.

"You can," said Mr. Vanderpuff.

"Then here goes," said Bridget.

She placed the base of the ladder firmly against the great, heavy table and leaped toward the bakery's vaulted ceiling, where sweet smells swirled in sumptuous clouds.

"Gotcha!" she cried, grabbing one of the cupcakes.

The little cake stuck fast.

"Well done, my dear!" said Mr. Vanderpuff. "Throw it down to me."

Bridget pulled so hard on the cupcake that her face turned beetroot red.

"I can't!" she gasped, swinging back and forth. "It . . . won't . . . budge!"

"Good heavens," said Mr. Vanderpuff.

The ladder rattled to the bakery floor.

"Ah," said Bridget.

"Hmm," said Mr. Vanderpuff. "Well, this is a pickle, isn't it?"

"Not at all," said Bridget. "I'm in complete control of the situation."

Mr. Vanderpuff looked at Bridget, dangling from

the ceiling on a vanilla cupcake, her chef whites lit so brightly by the winter sun that she resembled a gigantic lightbulb.

"You're sure?" he said.

"Yes."

"Don't need rescuing?"

"Nope."

"Anything in that hair of yours that might help?"

"Nope," said Bridget, after a moment.

Pascal settled himself against a bag of sugar, hands behind his head.

His face, Bridget saw, was *gleaming* with joy.

"You're doing great," said the elf, twirling his moustache.

"And without your paraskirt, you couldn't just drop down, of course."

"No," said Bridget, whose arms were beginning to ache.

A car rumbled past the bakery.

A gaggle of elderly ladies nattered along the pavement.

"Any ideas?" said Mr. Vanderpuff. "I could pass up the ladder and—"

"Hang on," said Bridget, stretching across the

arch of the ceiling to the nearest cupcake. "If I can reach this one, then..."

Her fist closed around the buttercream.

"Careful!" shouted Mr. Vanderpuff.

"I'm okay!" said Bridget. "And if I *twist* this one..."

She twisted the first cupcake in a clockwise direction.

At first, nothing happened. Then—with a slow, sticky ssshhhcclllup sound—the cupcake came free. Bridget swung like a monkey on a vine, and thudded the cupcake back into the ceiling.

"They're suction cupcakes!" she yelled. "Look!"

Twist, ssshhhcclllup
      Twist, ssshhhcclllup
            Twist, ssshhhcclllup

And, after a few seconds, she had monkey-swung her way across the ceiling and landed safely on top of the fridge.

"Amazing!" Mr. Vanderpuff clapped.

"Incredible!" said Pascal, settling on the great baker's shoulder.

Bridget, her fists covered in glutinous buttercream, bowed.

"These are *brilliant*!" she said.

"They really are," said Mr. Vanderpuff, putting the Suction Cupcakes carefully on the other side of the room and covering them with foil. "Perhaps not *entirely* edible yet, but we're making progress—this bake didn't scream and run away!"

Bridget's head dropped.

"I'm never going to get any of this right," she said.

"You will, my dear, you will!" Mr. Vanderpuff straightened her spine and puffed up her hat. "Why don't we try a real crowd-pleaser tomorrow—an easy-peasy classic?"

"You *promise* it's easy-peasy?"

"Absolutely."

"Easy-peasy for *me*?"

"*Yes*," said Mr. Vanderpuff, but with rather less conviction.

Pascal pulled a face that said: *nope!*

The rest of the day passed in a blur of customers[32] and flour. Bridget tidied up, swept the floors and greeted the bake shop's delighted patrons. When, finally, the last of them left, balancing their immaculate boxes in a teetering tower, Bridget picked up Pascal, went past the Locked and Secret Door, and climbed onto her wobbly chair in the kitchenette.

Mr. Vanderpuff was sipping another tiny coffee. His sleeves were rolled up, and there was a stripe of caramel on his forehead.

"Have you enjoyed today, my dear?" he said.

Bridget nodded.

"It was brilliant. It's like I get to share the customers' happiness."

Mr. Vanderpuff's eyes glowed through the steam from his cup.

"That, Bridget, is *precisely* how I feel. Thank you for all your hard work—the shop has never been tidier! You must be ready for your supper."

He handed her another Vanderpuff's box.

---

[32] Bridget had even met the librarian, Miss Paige, who wore high-laced boots and fluffy sweaters and smelled of flowers.

Bridget gasped.

She looked at the box. Its edges were as crisp as folded linen, and its golden letters seemed to glow in the kitchen's gentle light.

"Goodness!" she said, pulling the ribbon.

The Deelite's pastry was just as perfectly flaky, the cream as wonderfully smooth, the strawberries as excitingly sharp.

She could feel the *tingle* of it right in the tips of her hair.

"Feeling a little more settled tonight, my dear?"

"A little," said Bridget. "I'd be happier if I hadn't caused chaos in the bakery again."

"All good fun," said Mr. Vanderpuff, smiling widely. "Sleep well."

Bridget went to her Room of Bed, climbed into the Sentient Covers' cosy cocoon, and waited until Pascal was asleep.

Then, when the elf began to snore his tiny snores, she whispered, "I need to go to the bathroom."

The Covers fell away, and Bridget tiptoed into the hall.

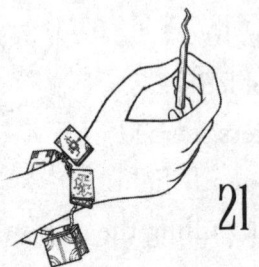

21

Lockpicking at Night

tRumping ✸ sneaking ✸ tRying

The Locked and Secret Door stood over her, a monolith of wood and paint and steel.

It felt heavy, like it was *pulling* her, like it was the center of the whole world, dragging the bakery, the village, the mountains and the seas toward it.

Bridget reached into her hair and spun the lockpicks between her fingers.

"All right," she said. "Let's do this."

"Bridget?"

Bridget jumped a foot in the air.

"Pascal?" she whispered, gasping for breath. "I

thought you were asleep!"

"I was," said the elf, yawning. "But I trumped myself awake again."

"I see."

"I've been quite windy this evening."

"I *know*," said Bridget, with feeling.

"Those aren't your usual shoes," said Pascal.

Bridget glanced down at her silk slippers.

"These are my Sneaky Sneaking Shoes.[33] This is how I moved round the Orphanage at night without Miss Acrid hearing me."

"Couldn't you just call those *sneakers*?"

"Well, yes, I suppose. All right—these are my Sneaky Sneakers. Better?"

"Definitely," said Pascal, patting his little tummy. "What are you doing?"

Bridget crouched in front of the keyhole.

"I'm picking the Locked and Secret Door," she said.

Pascal settled on the floor, his tiny head leaning against her knee.

"I know Mrs. Vanderpuff's portrait is in here,"

---

[33] For sneaking.

Bridget said, after a few minutes' patient work. "What else is there?"

"Oh, it's his inventing room," said Pascal drowsily.

Bridget's ears pricked up.

"He has an *inventing* room? What does he invent? Sneaking machines? Flying machines? *Time* machines?"

Pascal waved his hands.

"Cakes! He invents all the fabulous bakes for which his shop is so famous. All the Caramagnificents, the Fabananananas, the Deelites, *all* of them, were invented in that room."

Bridget tried a new pick.

"But it's been locked for a long time," she said.

"And he's invented nothing new," said Pascal, his eyes filling with tears. "Everything he ever made, he made for her. He wanted only for *her* to be impressed, to be proud of him. She was his muse and inspiration, and when she died, he put her picture inside and threw away the key. That was when he stopped seeing me—when he closed himself off from the world of magic."

Bridget settled back on her haunches.

"I thought he *lost* the key?"

Pascal shook his head, once.

"He only said that because it hurts him to think of it. No, in his heartbreak he threw the key in the River Belle. I swam down there myself to try to retrieve it—we elves are excellent swimmers—but the currents had already carried it out to sea."

"Oh," said Bridget. "So, the only way he'll ever get back in here is if *I* pick the lock?"

Pascal sighed sadly.

"You can't," he said. "So many others have tried—and none of them could do it."

"None of them," said Bridget, trying another pick, "was me."

The picks worked through the pins, shifted them, lifted them, played a little tune with them. She'd seen through the tips of her fingers every last inch of the ancient, iron mechanism, she knew exactly what she needed to do to open it.

But it wouldn't budge.

She glanced down. Pascal was asleep on her foot.

Two hours had passed as stealthily as a stalking cat.

Bridget sank to the floor, wrapped her arms round Pascal, and slept.

22

Razor Buns 1

As the morning rush began, Bridget had been stunned to be handed Mr. Vanderpuff's brass cake tongs.

"Are you sure?" she asked.

"Absolutely!" said Mr. Vanderpuff, as Pascal hopped with glee. "You can take the orders, too."

And she had: Chocolatte Bing Bongs, Fabanananana Swirls, Cheery Cherry Cheeriepops and Deelites by the baker's dozen.

It had been another wonderful morning.

She had woken in time to sneak back into bed, cradling the snoozing elf in her arms, and emerged from her Room of Bed as though she'd spent the whole night there, sleeping peacefully, instead of trying and failing to break into the Locked and Secret Door.

Behind which, she now knew, lay the secrets to Mr. Vanderpuff's incredible creativity.

As the customers filed through the bake shop, she laughed and smiled and felt about as happy as she could ever remember being.

Until it turned ten o'clock, when her tummy had started doing nervous flips.

"What are we making today?" she said now, blinking in the light from the high window.

Mr. Vanderpuff clapped his hands and dropped a bag of flour onto the table.

"Rock buns," he said. "They are very light, and very crumbly, and very nice with a cup of tea. I don't make them often, but whenever I do, they always sell out straight away. We're going to have a fabulous time making them. Good, sticky fun!"

"That sounds lovely," said Bridget. "But I think we got enough stickiness from the Suction Cupcakes, don't you?"

Pascal hid behind a mixing machine. His little elf eyes peeked out, then ducked back.

"These are only sticky while you're mixing them,"

said Mr. Vanderpuff firmly. "Don't you worry about a thing. Now, we start with a large bowl, to which we add flour, sugar and baking power. Then we mix in the butter."

He handed Bridget the bowl.

Bridget gripped it nervously.

"Mixing," she said, swirling the ingredients together. "Mixing. *Mixing*. To mix. Moving it all round and round. This is fine. I like mixing. *Mix*ing."

Mr. Vanderpuff nodded encouragingly.

"Next," he said, "we rub in the butter. We do it like this, between our thumbs and forefingers, so that it goes all breadcrumby, see?"

"It looks sticky," said Bridget.

"That's good. It'll stick the cakes together."

"Right," said Bridget. "Here I go..."

She plunged her hands into the bowl. The mixture was squidgy and soft and—she found, to her surprised delight—fun to squeeze.

Mr. Vanderpuff took his hands from his face.

"Oh," he said. "Well done! That looks super. Yes, indeed! We're on our way!"

"I *like* this!" said Bridget. "It's soothing."

"I've always thought that," beamed Mr.

Vanderpuff. "This part of the process is one of my favorites. *Look* at this — you're doing it perfectly!"

"Am I?" said Bridget.

"Yes!" cried Mr. Vanderpuff, as Pascal edged nervously back round the mixer. "I couldn't do it better myself! Let's mix in the raisins . . . Now, we need another bowl."

"What for?" asked Bridget, washing her hands in the big, trough-like sink.

"Our egg, milk and vanilla," said Mr. Vanderpuff, cracking an egg with his usual lightning speed. "Shall I whisk this together?"

"It's probably for the best," said Bridget sadly. "I don't want to do anything crazy. Again."

Mr. Vanderpuff nodded, then whisked the mixture into a frothy blur.

"Don't worry," he said, "we're nearly done now."

Bridget's eyebrows shot up.

"Really?"

Mr. Vanderpuff grinned.

"Really," he said.

"I've nearly made a cake?"

"You've nearly made

a *bun*," said Mr. Vanderpuff. "We just need to add the wet ingredients to the dry ingredients. So, we add this mixture," he handed Bridget the eggy milk, "to the one you've already mixed together."

Bridget held the bowl, poised to pour, in midair.

Mr. Vanderpuff and Pascal waited patiently.

A few more seconds passed.

"Is everything all right, my dear?" asked Mr. Vanderpuff.

"Come on!" said Pascal. "What's the worst that could happen?" He paused, then added, "Actually, best not think about that!"

"I just pour it in?" said Bridget, whose arm was beginning to stiffen.

"You just pour it in," said Mr. Vanderpuff. "Then we fold it together to make a dough."

"Fold it? Like a bedsheet?"

"Not quite. It means we sort of lift the spoon through it. Like this," Mr. Vanderpuff moved the spoon in a perfect folding motion, "and then we bake it."

"All right," said Bridget.

And she poured in the mixture.

Razor Buns 2

Mr. Vanderpuff covered his face with his hands.

The liquid landed with a splash. Then it formed an eggy puddle.

Bridget started to fold it through.

Mr. Vanderpuff removed his hands from his face.

"Oh," he said. "All right! We're done! Now, you just put them in the oven."

"That's it?"

"That's it. All you need to do—the *only* thing you need to do now—is put this *perfectly* made mixture into the oven, and you'll have done it. Just that final step left, and it's the simplest step in the entire world."

Bridget grinned.

"*This* I can do," she said.

"Ha!"

"Sssh," hissed Mr. Vanderpuff, then he looked surprised at himself. "Sorry, I thought I heard someone laughing . . . that's it, my dear, spoon the mixture onto the tray, then slide it into the oven . . . there!"

Bridget slammed the oven door.

"Is that it?" she said, giving Pascal a firm nod.

"That's it! You've done it!"

Bridget jumped up and clapped her hands.

"I've done it!" she cried. "I can't believe it!"

"All we do now is watch them rise. And once they've doubled in size, we'll take them out and have them with tea."

"And they'll definitely work? There's nothing that could go wrong?"

The sun beamed around Mr. Vanderpuff's head, making his eyes twinkle and shine.

"Nothing that I can think of," he said, giving her a wink.

Bridget pulled a stool over to the oven, and sat facing the glass door. The rock buns were already beginning to grow and swell, and their sweet aroma was blowing into the room on the oven's warm breeze.

"I'm going to sit here until they're ready," she said, pressing her knees together and folding her hands. "I've never been so excited in my entire life!"

"You sit there, my dear," said Mr. Vanderpuff, as Pascal flapped onto Bridget's shoulder. "I shall tidy this mess—and start brewing our tea!"

Bridget gave Pascal a broad grin.

"I've done it!" she whispered. "When these buns come out the oven, Mr. Vanderpuff will see that I can be a great baker, just like him. And when I pick the lock on the Locked and Secret Door—"

"Which you couldn't do," said Pascal.

"But I *will* do it, like I've baked these buns, and then I'll get Etta's portrait, get Mr. Vanderpuff back into his inventing room, make him see you again, and I'll stay here forever!"

"I believe you," said the elf. "You're a determined one, Bridget Baxter!"

Bridget took a deep breath of the sweet bun smell and felt a kick of excitement in her heart. Pascal sighed, and the bakery filled with the happy chime and splash of sudsy dishwashing.

"Mr. Vanderpuff!" Bridget shouted, standing so quickly she knocked over the stool. "I think that's it—I think they're ready!"

Mr. Vanderpuff hurried over and closed his eyes. He took a long, slow inhalation beside the oven door, a smile on his lips.

Then he stood bolt upright.

"What is it?" asked Bridget, her stomach clamping tight. "Is something wrong?"

"They smell . . ."

"Good? Bad? Terrible? Worse?"

". . . almost ready, but . . ."

"Oh *no*," moaned Bridget. "What have I done now?"

Mr. Vanderpuff stepped in front of her and retied his apron. His face was serious.

A bake was in trouble.

"I'm not sure what's going on, my dear," he said, rolling his shoulders as though preparing for combat. "But I *do* know this—there's something wrong with those buns."

He crouched down and opened the oven door.

The smell that filled the room was warm and inviting.

Bridget sniffed it in.

"They smell . . . fine, don't they?"

Mr. Vanderpuff shook his head.

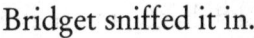

"I don't understand it," he muttered. "They *do* smell fine—and yet . . ."

"Sort of . . . sharp," said Pascal.

"What do you mean, sharp?" asked Bridget.

Mr. Vanderpuff nodded.

"That's exactly right," he said. "They smell *very* sharp."

Bridget, the heat from the oven blasting into her face, leaned forward.

She sniffed. The buns were warm and rich with a fruity, vanilla sweetness. She opened her eyes.

There was something else, something right on the edge of the aroma that seemed almost to cut her throat.

"They *look* good," she said, reaching over Mr. Vanderpuff's shoulder to lift one of the buns from the tray. "And if they *smell* good enough to eat, then—"

Mr. Vanderpuff grabbed her wrist.

"Wait," he said.

He lifted the nearest bun and, holding it as

though it was very fragile and delicate, ran it along the big table.

A sliver of wood, as thin as snakeskin, peeled from the table's surface and fluttered to the floor.

"*Wow*," breathed Bridget. "That *is* sharp."

"As a razor," said Mr. Vanderpuff.

"Good grief!" said Pascal, gasping in shock and wonderment. "Just when I think you've made a normal bake, you go and make something *even more incredible—again*!"

"I've made *razor* buns?" said Bridget. She picked up one of the buns as carefully as she could. The edge shimmered in the sunlight, sharp as a samurai sword. "We can't eat these!"

"Not unless we want them to slice through our tummies and land on our feet," said Mr. Vanderpuff.

Bridget held the bun close to her face.

"Maybe if we—*aaaaaargh*! My nose!" She threw the razor bun high in the air, sending Mr. Vanderpuff and Pascal scrambling for cover. "Oh, no! Don't worry, I'll—"

"Don't catch it!" shouted Mr. Vanderpuff from below a steel trolley. "It'll cut you in half! Get under here!"

Bridget dived in beside him—as the razor bun thudded into the table like an arrow.

"Oh, *no!*" said Bridget, covering her face with her hands.

Mr. Vanderpuff pried them gently apart. His hands were soft and warm, and when she looked up, she found his twinkling eyes.

"The villagers think I've got magic in these hands, you know. But they're wrong—it's not magic, it's hard work. There's no spell book, no incantation that makes things taste as good as they do—just me, trying and failing over and over until I get it right."

"I think I can only do the failing part," said Bridget, dabbing the cut on her nose.

"Then we shall keep doing that *together*, and for as long as you wish. Let's try one more time, shall we? And let's not wait until tomorrow—we'll do it tonight."

"*Tonight?*"

"This very night."

Bridget took a deep breath.

"Is it something else easy-peasy?"

"The easiest and peasiest," said Mr. Vanderpuff. "*Jelly.*"

24

Jellymite 1

The afternoon whooshed past in a pleasant blur: more customers, more cakes, more happy, smiling faces. Vanderpuff's shelves emptied, the big brass till sang—and the people of Belle-on-Sea toddled home for an evening of comfortable deliciousness.

Bridget and Mr. Vanderpuff supped on a buttery Crumple Crumpet, changed into their chef's pajama whites[34]—complete with night cap and slippers—then headed for the kitchen.

Snowflakes were dropping like sparks through

---

[34] Mr. Vanderpuff, struck frequently in the night by both inspiration and the low beam over his bed, was always properly attired when whisking in the wee hours.

the streetlight in the oval window, and the village's sleepiness drifted over the cobbles like fog.

Bridget felt sure they must be the only people awake in the whole of Belle-on-Sea, their warm lamp a solitary candle among the nighttime blue.

She wiggled her toes.

They were working at a steel trolley. Mr. Vanderpuff had wheeled it next to the mixing table, which still had a razor bun sticking out from its surface.

"Now," said Mr. Vanderpuff, in a voice that suggested he was pleading with his own mind, "jelly really *is* simple—it is! It's simply a matter of counting."

"Counting?" said Bridget. "Like maths?"

"Exactly! We count how much water we use, and that tells us how much gelatin we need. If we get those numbers right, we get the jelly right!"

Bridget felt a skip of excitement.

"I'm good at maths," she said.

"Then you will be good at jelly," said Mr. Vanderpuff firmly.

But Bridget heard the doubt in the great baker's tone.

"First," said Mr. Vanderpuff, "we put our gelatin leaves in water."

"What *is* gelatin?"

"It's like a sort of glue for cooking. It's what makes the jelly wobbly."

"So, it's important?"

"Very. And it's also important we put all five leaves in one at a time."

"Why?" asked Bridget. She laid each leaf in the bowl of water, watching as they drifted below the surface.

"If we throw them all in at once, they might stick together. This is where great baking *really* happens, my dear—in the details!"

The final gelatin leaf drifted through the water and settled in the bowl.

"What do we do next?"

"We add our sugar," said Mr. Vanderpuff, handing Bridget another small bowl, "into this pan of water. Then we stir it every so often."

Bridget lifted the spoon.

Mr. Vanderpuff and Pascal threw themselves under the table.

"Like this?" said Bridget, stirring gently.

The sugar began to dissolve, vanishing into the bubbles.

"Um . . . yes," said Mr. Vanderpuff, brushing himself down and trying to act like a man who hadn't just dived for cover. "Sorry, I tripped over. Clumsy me."

"I also tripped," said Pascal.

Mr. Vanderpuff returned to his position at Bridget's shoulder.

"Well done!" he cried, clapping happily. "The sugar has dissolved, so now we can add the raspberries."

The clouds shifted. A shaft of moonlight cut the bakery in half, and the steam from Bridget's pot curled through its wintery glow. The only sounds to be heard were the pot-bubbles *hissing*, the wooden spoon *clonking* and the Scream Cream snoring gently in the fridge.

Bridget tipped the raspberries into the water.

Mr. Vanderpuff leaped under the table, Pascal at his heels.

The raspberries settled in the bottom of the pot. Bridget stirred them.

"It's working!" she said excitedly. "It's really working!"

"Um . . . yes," said Mr. Vanderpuff. "Sorry, I tripped. Again."

"What about you, Pascal?" Bridget whispered.

Pascal shuffled his feet.

"Actually," he said, "I thought I might be in terrible, raspberry-based danger."

"Fair enough," said Bridget.

"We let this come to the boil," said Mr. Vanderpuff,

leaning over the pot. "Then give it a few minutes with the heat turned down."

"Do I keep stirring?"

"Only a little. It'll be hot enough in there to mash the raspberries up nicely. I say, this is going rather well, isn't it?"

"Yes," said Bridget. "It really is. I like this kind of baking."

"So do I," said Mr. Vanderpuff.

"Glorious!" said Pascal. "I must be the happiest Butters in the world!"

A minute passed in companionable silence. The baker, the elf and Bridget watched bubbles break on the sides of the pot.

"Let's add the gelatin," said Mr. Vanderpuff, handing the bowl to Bridget. "Then we add our final ingredient and put it in the fridge."

"What's the final ingredient?" asked Bridget, slipping the leaves of gelatin into the pot.

"Lemon juice."

Bridget gasped.

"But lemons are sour and horrible!" she said.

"That may be," replied Mr. Vanderpuff, handing her an enormous, bright lemon. "But they're full of useful things that make bakes delicious. We cut it open, like so," he took hold of Bridget's hands, and together they cut the lemon in half, "and *gently* squeeze some juice into the pot."

Bridget had never touched a lemon before. Its skin was very firm, and very bumpy.

"All right," she said, taking the fruit between thumb and forefinger. "Gently does it . . ."

She squeezed the lemon.

Jellymite 2

The wedge of lemon disappeared in her fist, as though crushed by a steel trap. A torrent of juice sluiced into the pot. The liquid sizzled and spat—then began to swell.

"I said a *gentle* squeeze!" wailed Mr. Vanderpuff, grabbing Bridget and diving back under the trolley.

Bridget tucked Pascal under her arm. The pot hissed like a serpent, the jelly inside swelling like a giant, red mushroom.

"I didn't mean it!" shouted Bridget, lifting her head above the trolley. "I promise I only squeezed a tiny bit!"

"Stay down!" yelled Mr. Vanderpuff.

"I think it's okay!" Bridget yelled back, as a big, red drop fell from the pot's rim. "I don't think it's dangero—"

BOOM!

The *instant* the jelly drop touched the trolley, a huge explosion flashed in Bridget's face, knocking her to the floor.

A spatula juddered next to her with a cacophonous *drrroooing*.

More drops formed on the sides of the pot—then fell.

BOOM! BOOM! BOOM! BOOM!

"It's like dynamite!" cried Mr. Vanderpuff, throwing himself across Bridget to protect her from falling kitchenware. Pascal dodged between the flashing explosions like a panicked hen, his mouth wide and screaming.

Bridget met Mr. Vanderpuff's eyes.

"It's Jellymite!" they screamed together.

BOOM! BOOM!

"It'll wake up the whole village!" shouted Mr. Vanderpuff, pressing his night cap to his head. "We need to get it into a jar!"

"Right, good plan! Where are they?"

"In the cupboard on the other side of the bakery!"

Bridget followed Mr. Vanderpuff's pointing hand. She stood—just as a rolling pin hit the wall and burst into a thousand splinters.

"No!" cried Mr. Vanderpuff, clutching her hand. "Let me go—it's too dangerous!"

"I'll be fine!" called Bridget, reaching into her hair and withdrawing a pair of safety goggles. "It'll be like the time I put beetles in Miss Acrid's slippers. Only without the sandwich cannon," she added.

"The what? I don't underst—" Mr. Vanderpuff began.

But Bridget was already moving, rolling under another incoming rolling pin and leaping over a puddle of flaming Jellymite before landing beside the cupboard with a thud.

"You did it!" called Mr. Vanderpuff, his voice almost drowned out. "Get a glass jar with a lid—if

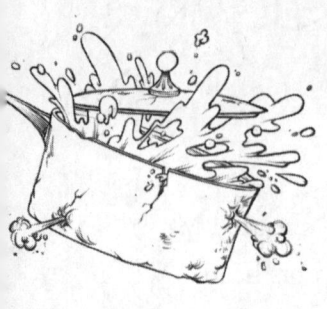

we tip the Jellymite in there, it should stop the explosions!"

Bridget rummaged through the cupboard's shelves, throwing ramekins and pots and plastic containers over her shoulder until, in the flash of the biggest Jellymite explosion yet, she saw the jars Mr. Vanderpuff had described.

"That's them!" cried the baker as she held one up. "One, two, three!"

Together, they jumped toward the pot and, keeping their faces far from the spurts of flame, tipped the Jellymite into the biggest jar.

Bridget snapped the lid closed—and the explosions stopped.

They stood, panting with exertion and terror, listening to the sudden, shocking silence.

"Well," said Mr. Vanderpuff, his eyebrows smoking softly. "That's another new one."

"Has anyone ever made Jellymite before?" asked Bridget.

Mr. Vanderpuff shook his head. His face was blackened with soot, and his hair stood on end.

"Not to my knowledge," he said. Then, seeing

Bridget's expression, added brightly, "A world first!"

Bridget wrinkled her nose.

"I don't *want* a world first," she said. "I just want to bake cakes people could eat, instead of things they could take into battle."

"Yes," said Mr. Vanderpuff, looking around the bakery. Pieces of silver cookware studded the walls and floor like the spines of a great hedgehog. "I understand."

The jar containing the Jellymite gave a *pop*. Pascal leaped into Bridget's arms, and promptly fainted.

Bridget looked at her lovely new chef's pajama whites, now spattered and stained and scorched with exploding berries.

"Well, my dear," said Mr. Vanderpuff, dabbing at his forehead with a dishcloth. "That was quite an experience. I think, perhaps, we should have some supper. Are you hungry?"

Bridget looked up and saw Mr. Vanderpuff's twinkling eyes—saw him still smiling amid the chaos and ruin of his bakery.

"I'm always hungry for Vanderpuff's food," she said, carrying the unconscious elf into the bake shop.

26

Supper

soup ✳ Etta's story ✳ love

Bridget took another spoonful. The soup was rich and hot in her tummy, and almost sticky on her lips.

"This is wonderful," she said. "What's that sort of . . . *warm* flavor?"

"Paprika," said Mr. Vanderpuff. "This is Etta's *soup d'amour*. I can't make it as well as she did, but it makes me think of her, so I eat it often."

Bridget looked around the kitchen's happy, steamy warmth and imagined Etta Vanderpuff, covered in the bakery's floury clouds, smiling as she placed her husband's soup in front of him.

Somehow, she had told him to bring Bridget here.

But why me? Bridget thought. *Mr. Vanderpuff has given me chance after chance, and instead of baking lovely cakes, I just keep blowing everything up.*

"Why so glum, chum?" said Pascal.

"Because," Bridget whispered, her lips as still as statues, "I took my time, I followed the recipes, I *really* watched Mr. Vanderpuff and tried to copy everything he did. But I'm missing something."

"It'll come," said Pascal. "Be patient."

Bridget nodded.

But she knew, deep down, that the little elf was wrong.

Something was painfully obvious: Mr. Vanderpuff really *understood* baking.

He knew his mixture was ready simply by *listening* to it, and he could *smell* his sponge was done through an oven door. He *sensed* exactly when the right moment had come to bring his bakes out into the world.

She had tried to do the same thing. She had closed her eyes. She had *tried* to smell and sense and *feel*.

And she had succeeded only in ruining *everything*.

"I'm rubbish at baking, aren't I?" she said aloud.

Pascal glanced up, his jaws frozen in the act of biting a Pistachio Pi-Pie.[35]

Mr. Vanderpuff tilted his head to one side.

"Why would you say that, my dear? You'd never baked before, I don't think you've done badly at all."

"Mr. Vanderpuff, I have egg on my face."

"There's no need to feel embarrassed, it's only you and I who—"

"*Actual* egg, Mr. Vanderpuff," said Bridget, unsticking her hair, "there are yolks behind my ears."

Mr. Vanderpuff took another mouthful of soup.

"That could happen to anyone."

Bridget fixed him with a very focused look.

"I've been here for three days," she said, "and I've completely destroyed your bakery, taken a chunk out of your table with a supposedly soft bun, burned off your eyebrows, and instead of delicious cakes, I've baked a bunch of sticking, screaming,

---

[35] Always *perfectly* circular, Pistachio Pi-Pies are very popular with maths teachers.

slicing, *exploding* things that wouldn't so much satisfy a customer's hunger as make them armed and dangerous."

Mr. Vanderpuff lifted his bowl with both hands, drank the last of his soup, then wiped his mouth with the back of his hand.

"Ah!" he said. "It's quite true, Bridget—you've done all those things. And have you enjoyed yourself?"

Bridget blinked, then squeezed her empty thumb.

"Yes," she said, thinking guiltily of Tom. "They've been the best three days of my entire life."

Mr. Vanderpuff smiled and tapped the tip of her nose with his spoon.

"Do you know what *soup d'amour* means?" he asked.

"Yes," said Bridget. "It means the soup of love."

Mr. Vanderpuff smiled, painfully, as though trying to keep his emotions under control.

"That's right. My wife, my darling Etta, used to make it for me whenever I had a particularly difficult day in the bakery. She understood me. We shared everything with each other."

"Including your dreams?" said Bridget.

A tear glistened in the corner of Mr. Vanderpuff's eye.

"Especially the dreams," he said.

Bridget slurped some more soup. She could feel its glow reaching to the farthest tips of her hair.

"Tell me about Etta," she said.

The air between them seemed to hang, suspended, as though a curtain had dropped to close Mr. Vanderpuff away—then he leaned forward, and the curtain lifted.

"She was wonderful," he said. "Quick to laugh, quick to cry. Smart as a whip, too—she always knew how to fix things, and how to make me feel better. If I was ever in a grump, she would cheer me up like a shot."

"I can't imagine you being grumpy," said Bridget.

"Oh, of course I can be grumpy! We all can. Sometimes it's fun to stay in a bad mood, and stomp around the place. Sometimes I wanted to be left to stew and boil in my own juices and get grumpier and grumpier. But Etta wouldn't have it. She'd hug me and look into my eyes. And once I saw her . . . well, I couldn't be anything but happy, because I had her beside me, and we were loving each other and looking after each other and that was that."

Bridget ate some soup. A tear fell into her bowl. "Tell me more," she said.

Mr. Vanderpuff sat back in his chair. He was smiling now.

"She got freckles on her nose in summertime. She used to cut her hair short, then decide she missed it being long, so grew it back—then cut it all off again. She loved fruit, and milkshakes—I used to make her the best milkshakes you've ever tasted, with honey and strawberries and melon and papaya and everything else you can imagine. When we danced in the kitchen, she used to spin her dress around her legs. When we hugged, she fit just under my chin, and I would smell her hair and kiss her right on the top of the head. It was as though she held a piece of my soul, and I a piece of hers. We were a little team, and we loved each other so much."

He blinked, and tears fell down his cheeks. "Her skin smelled sweet, like coconut. Her hair smelled of cherry bark and almonds."

Bridget wiped her eyes.

"What happened to her?" she asked.

Pascal settled on Mr. Vanderpuff's shoulder. The great baker, without realizing what he was doing, nuzzled into the elf and closed his eyes.

Pascal kissed his forehead.

"She was giving birth to our first child," said Mr. Vanderpuff. "Something went wrong, and I—" He took a deep breath. "I lost them both. Sometimes I think a part of me died with them. Sometimes I think *all* of me did, and that I can never be whole again. And now, of course, her lovely portrait is gone forever—trapped behind the Locked and Secret Door. But she still comes to me in my dreams. Without those dreams, I think I would be lost entirely."

"Like the dream where she told you about me?"

Mr. Vanderpuff wiped his tears on his sleeve.

"Exactly like that. In the dream, I was sitting in this very seat, and she was sitting where you are. She took my hands and told me that I was going to do something very important—far more important than baking and cakes and chocolate."

"What could be more important than your

baking?" said Bridget.

Mr. Vanderpuff's eyes twinkled through his tears.

"You," he said simply. "Making sure you were happy and loved for the rest of your life."

Pascal blew Bridget a kiss.

"You're one of us now!" He clapped. "My wonderful friend!"

Bridget let go a sob that was also a laugh, an explosion of noise that made her heart skip in her chest and made her laugh some more.

"I'll get Etta's portrait back, Mr. V," she said. "I swear it."

Mr. Vanderpuff ruffled her hair.

"Don't you worry about that," he said. "Just you—"

"I mean it," said Bridget, wiping her eyes. "One time, Miss Acrid locked Tom in a sack, put him in a big chest and wrapped *that* in chains, then threw him in the lake. I had him out and drying in the sun before she even realized I had escaped from the dungeon."

Mr. Vanderpuff shook his head.

"For the life of me," he said, "I can't fathom why an Orphanage even *needs* a dungeon. But it's not

Etta's portrait you should be thinking about—it's Tom's ring."

Bridget looked down. She was gripping the thumb with the missing ring so hard the skin had turned white.

"Oh," she said.

"I see you doing that," said Mr. Vanderpuff, "like you're doing now."

Bridget let her thumb go.

"I always had him with me," she said, "in the Orphanage. And everything was all right, even when it wasn't, even when the Families came and we were never chosen, it was all right because we were together."

Mr. Vanderpuff nodded.

"If I have learned anything about life, my dear," he said, "it's that family is the most important thing in the whole world. You can gather all the money and power, but without *love* your life will be completely and utterly meaningless. You shared your life with Tom, just as you shared that stolen croissant. But the most precious thing he had to give was not a ring— he gave you his friendship, and his love. *That's* the thing that matters most. And with that," he finished, rising and stretching, "I think we shall go to bed. We have another big day tomorrow."

"What's tomorrow's lesson?" asked Bridget, yawning.

Mr. Vanderpuff smiled.

"We're going back to where your journey with baked goods began—the *croissant*."

"Goodness," said Bridget, her eyes widening. Pascal climbed onto her shoulder. "That does sound like fun."

"I wonder how you'll manage to make a soft, flaky croissant dangerous?" whispered the elf with a chuckle.

"Oh," said Bridget, glancing at the Locked and Secret Door, "I'm sure I'll manage."

Part Four
Kidnap

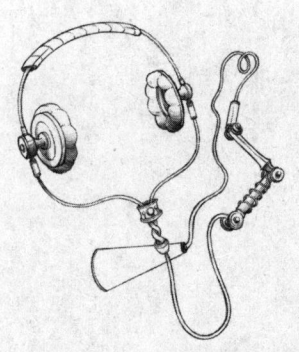

27

Snap

sneaking ✷ lockpicking ✷ bRoken picks

Bridget tried not to go to sleep, but the Sentient Covers curled and snuggled and smooshed around her and she woke hours later, drooling in her upside-down floating starfish position.

Pascal was snoozing on his back, his mouth moving noiselessly as he dreamed.

The only sounds in the world were the whisper of wind against the roof, and the soft *click* of the elf's teeth.

Bridget looked at the ceiling and thought about the dream she'd been having.

She'd been in the bakery. There had been a little

cabinet, with a single drawer. And when she put her hand inside, she'd woken up.

She imagined Tom was with her, the comforting brightness of his eyes looking into hers, and squeezed the place the ring should have been.

Here, in the darkness, the events of the last few days seemed to possess the same quality as her dream; all the smells and sounds of the exploding, screaming, sticky bakes were like some imagined fantasy.

And yet, she reminded herself, they had happened. She really had whipped cream into a screaming blob, monkey-swung along the ceiling on vanilla cupcakes, sliced into a table with a bun, and turned a bakery into a war zone with nothing more than a bowlful of jelly.

She smiled.

"I need to go to the bathroom!" she whispered.

The Sentient Covers freed her in an instant.

Pascal cracked open one eye, then yawned.

"Again?" he said.

"Of course," said Bridget. "And I'm going to do it this time, too."

"*Really?*" said the elf. "Mind if I stay here?"

"Suit yourself," said Bridget. She reached into her hair, took out her lockpicks, then tied her reluctant curls into a ponytail. "But I'd hate for you to miss it."

Pascal climbed groggily onto her shoulder.

"Oh, all *right*," he said, yawning. "Couldn't you just be determined and heroic during the *day*time?"

Bridget spun the lockpicks round her finger, then stepped into the hallway.

"Let's go," she said.

The flat was still. Mr. Vanderpuff's bedroom door was closed, and all the lights were off. Bridget glanced at the empty space where Etta's portrait had hung and pressed her fingers gently to the wall.

She could almost feel the picture below her, trapped behind the Locked and Secret Door, glowing with the love Mr. and Mrs. Vanderpuff had shared.

Bridget slipped on her Sneaky Sneakers and ghosted down the hall, moving like a shadow through the darkness, her hair floating behind like a big, curly cloud. Moonlight poured through the skylight onto the polished floor, making white bars of light between which Bridget placed her silent feet, like a cat picking its way along a fence.

She leaped, without stopping, onto the banister and zoomed down once more into the heart of the bakery, landing with a soundless roll right in front of the Locked and Secret Door.

"Right, Pascal—I'm going to pick this lock, *tonight*. And once I'm in, I'm going to take Etta's picture back upstairs and hang it in its space. Mr. V will get the nicest surprise ever when he sees it in the morning!"

"Dear girl," said the elf, "we've been over this, even you, with all your determination can't *possibly*—"

"I can," Bridget interrupted. "And I will."

"All right," said the elf. "Wake me once you're inside."

Bridget watched as he fell asleep, then took a deep breath and slid her tweezle-tip from its case.

"Here we go," she said, closing her eyes, letting her mind drift back into the skin of her lockpicking hand until she existed only as a brain and the five little antennas of her fingertips, each listening attentively to the coded whispers of the great, unyielding lock.

She twisted and turned, finding the hills and valleys of the metal inside, following the raindrop patter of shifting pins, *lifting* and *turning* the tweezle-tip so they began to dance in a soft, chiming rhythm.

Without opening her eyes, she reached into her hair and withdrew the hook-tip pick, slotting it in and *lifting* it just so, and the pitch of the lock's voice changed slightly, a tensing as though it wanted to shout, to sing, to spill its secrets.

The lock was old and heavy, and the pressure of the pins was leaving a deep dent in her skin. She carried on twisting and tickling and tapping, working her way toward the movement that would break it apart.

All those people who tried before, she thought, *the locksmith and the thief and the men with axes — they didn't want the door to open, not the way I do. That's why I'm going to do it.*

She swapped back to the tweezle-tip, and carried on.

"*Mmmmffffll?*" said Pascal, half dreaming.

"Sometimes it takes longer," Bridget said, her eyes

still closed. "But I *can* do it."

She pushed the curling-tip pick alongside the tweezle-tip, and began to *twist* them *together*, all the while pushing *up* as hard as she could, so that her arms began to shake and the sweat prickled on her brow.

"Come on . . ." she whispered, as Pascal prised open an eye and pushed himself onto his elbows. "This is it, this *has* to be it, Mr. V *needs* this to—work!"

She gave a final, massive *heave*.

And the lockpicks snapped.

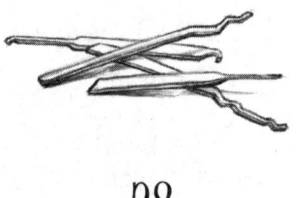

28

Dreams

Bridget's dream ✳ Etta's portrait ✳ broken glass

Bridget fell to her knees.

"No!" she gasped, scrambling to retrieve the picks from the floor, holding them together as though they might still be of use, might still be capable of breaking the door's fearsome lock. "I *need* to get Etta's picture back for Mr. V! He deserves it! I can't bake his cakes, but I've *always* been able to pick locks, and this was going to be the only thing I could do for him!"

She grabbed two fistfuls of hair and buried her face in them.

"Mr. V deserves better than me, Pascal," she said,

after a minute of silent tears. "I can't keep ruining things for him, especially if the *one* thing I've always been able to do doesn't even—"

She froze.

"What is it?" asked Pascal.

"Hang on," said Bridget.

"Can you hear something?" said Pascal nervously, settling on her shoulder.

"Yes," said Bridget, opening the door to the bake shop and tiptoeing toward the enormous, plate glass windows. "It sounds like . . . clomping."

The window exploded.

A blast of cold air struck Bridget, the blinds billowing in the breeze from the open, shattered frame. Shards of glass were strewn in a galaxy of bright slivers, reflecting the light of the moon in a fractured blur. The sweet, lavender smell of Belle-on-Sea filled the room as the outside rushed in, and the blinds fell to the floor.

Bridget peered through the chaos.

There, standing stock-still in the center of the broken pane, was Miss Acrid.

The moonlight at her back cast her face in shadow, but there could be no mistaking the set of her shoulders, the air of roiling menace, or the fact that she was wielding a sword shaped like a salmon.

She spotted Bridget among the debris, and her eyes flashed.

"There you are, *Baxter*!" she cried. "Still wearing your little sneaky sneak shoes, I see!"

Where is Mr. V? thought Bridget. *The sound of breaking glass should have had him charging downstairs in his chef's pajama whites.*

"You're a long way from the Orphanage, Acrid," she growled, brushing the glass from her hair. "I thought you never went beyond the gates."

"Unless I want something badly enough," said Miss Acrid, her eyes narrowing.

Bridget tensed her muscles.

"What do you want?" she asked.

The Mistress pointed to the brick lying in the middle of the shop.

There was a scrap of paper tied to it with a length of string.

"You didn't need to involve Mr. Vanderpuff in this!" Bridget shouted as she unwrapped the note. "This is between you and me!"

Miss Acrid pulled back her lips, showing her

brown, horsey teeth.

"I wasn't expecting to see you," she said. "But now I'll get the satisfaction of watching your rancid little *face* as you read!"

"What does it say?" asked Pascal, clinging, trembling, to Bridget's sleeve.

Hello, you stinky witch! You thought you'd gotten away, didn't you? You thought you'd seen the last of me!

Well, I have your precious Vandalscruff in my dungeon, and he's going to stay there forever. He came looking for Timpson's ring, but I caught him and now he's my prisoner.

This is what you get for crossing me!

Don't even try to rescue him—I have booby-trapped the entire Orphanage, so much so that even a poisonous sneak like you, with all your silly "inventions," couldn't ever get inside. You will never see him again, and his so-called bakery will rot into the ground because I'm going to make him bake ME cakes and pies and pastries forever, only me and nobody else, until all my tooths fall out.

Your "new life" is all ruined and it's your own fault, so yah-boo-sucks to you, you stinky little fart.

Miss Acrid

PS I wiped a bogey on this letter. I hope it's already stuck to your hand.

Bridget looked up.

Miss Acrid had melted into the darkness.

Bridget heard Mr. Vanderpuff's little car roaring back toward the Orphanage.

She felt giddy with the wrongness of everything: the Mistress's bogey on her wrist,[36] the broken,

---

[36] Miss Acrid was terribly fond of hiding bogeys in places people were likely to touch: letters, shoelaces, door handles, and sometimes even their own pockets.

shattered glass, the cold air in Mr. Vanderpuff's warm, cozy shop.

She ran up the stairs, taking the steps two at a time and bursting through the door of Mr. Vanderpuff's bedroom.

The room was very neat, and very plain. The chef's whites for the next day had been hung on the door.

The bed was empty. The curtains were drawn.

"He really is gone," said Bridget, her heart pounding. "Mr. V went to the Orphanage to get Tom's ring for me, and Miss Acrid locked him in the dungeon. He's got no way of getting out. She's right—he'll be stuck there forever."

"Oh, no!" screamed Pascal, nervously fanning his face. "What are we going to do?"

"The only thing we can do," said Bridget, crushing the note in her fist. "We're going to get him back."

She turned to go, and saw—at the side of the bed with the undented, unslept-on pillow—the little cabinet she had seen in her dream, just before she woke.

"It wasn't *just* a dream," she said. "It's Etta's bedside cabinet!"

29

Etta Vanderpuff

hair clip ✷ Etta's portrait ✷ a plan

"It's here," said Bridget. "It's really here! She must have *meant* for me to dream about it!"

"About what?" asked Pascal, hopping nervously on the carpet.

"About this!" said Bridget, running round the bed.

She dropped to her knees, hardly daring to touch the handle.

Then she imagined Etta's hand reaching for it, took a deep breath.

And opened the drawer.

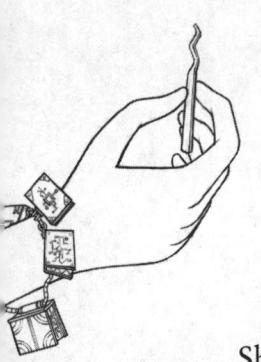

To anyone else, it would have seemed empty, cleared out by Mr. Vanderpuff as he tidied away his wife's things.

But Bridget was good at finding things.

She pulled the drawer out farther—and saw the hair clip in the deepest, darkest corner.

"Yes!" she cried, holding it aloft. "This is it, Pascal, this is how I get her portrait back!"

"By tidying up your hair?" said the elf, dazed and confused.

"By picking that lock!" cried Bridget, leaping onto the banister and flying toward the ground floor.

"*Now?* But you said we were going to rescue Mr. V!"

"We are," said Bridget, kneeling in front of the Locked and Secret Door. "*All* of him."

She kissed the hairpin, and bowed her head.

"This is it, Etta," she whispered.

And she slid the hairpin into the lock.

She thought about all the locks she'd picked over the years, all the times she'd pulled her picks from her hair after jumping off the roof or climbing from the dungeon or outsmarting Miss Acrid. She'd been escaping, or finding things for the other Childs, trinkets that were often the only things they had to remind them of their lost parents—the only things they owned that were truly *theirs*.

And Miss Acrid had taken them.

Bridget had been proud she was able to get them back—proud she had the skill to go up against the Mistress, and win.

Every picked lock, she realized now, every retrieval of a lost or stolen thing, had been leading up to this moment—the moment where she was able to do something for Etta and Ernest Vanderpuff that nobody else had been able to do.

She would open the door that had been closed for so long.

She would give Mr. V back his joy, as he had done for her.

Bridget gasped.

The lock was whispering its secret song, very faintly. But it wasn't the normal sound she was hearing, the usual song of pings and clicks.

It was a woman's gentle voice, telling her which way to turn, which way to twist—and when to push with all her might.

"It's Etta's voice," Bridget whispered.

And she *heaved* on the hairpin one final time.

With a cacophonous, heavy clonk, the lock's pins spun together, and the handle dropped.

Bridget stood before the wide-open Locked and Secret Door.

There was a picture-sized package leaning against a mixing table, wrapped in brown paper.

And everywhere, under soft, white dust sheets, were the machines and bowls of Mr. Vanderpuff's inventing room.

Bridget unwrapped the portrait.

Etta Vanderpuff's face was exactly as she'd imagined. She had shining brown hair, neatly tied in a ponytail, with bright eyes and a kind smile.

Bridget had an intense feeling of recognition, as though she'd seen her before, as though they'd been friends a long time ago.

"Hello," she said, aloud. "Mr. V misses you so much. I can see why."

"There she is," said Pascal, touching Etta's face. "What beauty. Such light in her eyes."

Bridget turned on the lamp and checked the clock.

"Right," she said. "Pascal, is there something that

could get us to the Orphanage *quickly*—another car, or a glider... *anything* that would be faster than running?"

Pascal looked blank and shook his head. Then his eyebrows shot up.

"There's an old messenger bike in the yard. It's a bit rusty, but it should work."

"Excellent," said Bridget, tying on an apron. "It's just past midnight, so there's still time to rescue Mr. Vanderpuff and be back here for breakfast."

"Is there?" said Pascal. "But how? You said he's imprisoned in a dungeon!"

"I've got out of that dungeon hundreds of times," said Bridget, rolling up her sleeves.

"Bridget! Listen to yourself—this is impossible!"

"No, it's not! Did Matilda think frightening the Trunchbull was impossible? Did Sherlock think beating Moriarty was impossible? Never! But this isn't going to be easy. The only way to get to Mr. V is through Miss Acrid's office. The note says she's set booby traps everywhere, and she'll be on the lookout. Luckily, I'm good at *everything*."

"But you're not good at everything!" screamed the elf, wringing his hands and pulling his ears. "You're an *awful* baker! I'm sorry, but you are! And if—"

Bridget silenced him with a finger on his lips, then took a bowl from a shelf.

"You're looking at it the wrong way," she said. "Nobody in the entire world is a *better* bad baker than me. And if I'm going to be bad," she brandished a whisk and narrowed her eyes, "I'm going to be *terrible*."

30
Miss Acrid Feels Confident

imprisonment ✶ greed ✶ family

The moonlight gleamed on the jar of eyeballs, newly arranged on its mended shelf, and caught the swirls of dust traveling between the office's hideous things.

"These buns really are *super*," said Miss Acrid.

She had taken off her gigantic, clomping boots. They sat, steaming, in the center of her enormous desk, like a hot-run engine cooling down.

"Delishush," said the Mistress, through a mouthful of dough. "I can't believe it took me so long to get round to kidnapping you," she went on, waving a Caramagnificent Donut like a conductor's baton. "All this, on tap, forever! Who shall we kidnap next? A burger whizz? A pizza chef? There's plenty of space in the dungeon... to think I wasted all those years on the Childs, when I could have been collecting an army of cooks to *feed* me whenever I want! Soon I'll have the finest restaurant there is, right under my foots!"

She stamped over to the trapdoor.

"You hear that, Vanderfoof?" she screamed, her voice echoing against the dungeon walls. "I'm going to get you some friends to play with!"

There was a pause. Then, as though whispered on a distant wind, came Mr. Vanderpuff's gentle voice.

"I'd rather go home, if it's all the same to you, Miss Acrid."

Miss Acrid threw back her head and shrieked her seagull's laugh.

"Home? You *are* home—you're going to stay down there for the rest of your life! And you'd better start thinking of fancy new cakes to send up here. I want to eat things no one has ever eaten before—cakes and bakes that don't exist anywhere else in the entire world!"

There was silence for a moment.

"No," said Mr. Vanderpuff. "I don't think I will. I think Bridget Baxter will come and save me."

"*Baxter?*" cried Miss Acrid. "Ha! Why would that little wretch come for *you*?"

"Because I love her," said Mr. Vanderpuff. "And I think she loves me, too. The second she set foot in my bakery, she became family. And you don't turn your back on family."

"*Family,*" snorted Miss Acrid, then wiped her nose. "You just keep making me fancy cakes, and forget about Bridget *Baxter*—she's got no chance against my booby traps! No chance at all!"

Far below her feet, Ernest Vanderpuff loaded another tray of Chocolatte Bing Bongs into the makeshift oven.

"We'll see," he said, smiling. "We'll see."

31

Bridget's Return

utility belt ✷ cycling ✷ tooled up

The moon, now higher in the sky, shone down on Vanderpuff's Bake Shop. Its pale light sparkled on the scattered diamond of the broken window and gathered in the blinds flapping in the wind.

The smell of snow, cold and bright, filled the space. Drifts of it had gathered on the display shelves, now exposed to the outside world.

A foot crunched on the glass.

Bridget—a utility belt around her waist, straps about her shoulders—emerged onto Candlewick Place.

After two hours of frantic baking, she had flour in her hair, cream in her ears, sugar in her shoes.

And fire in her belly.

The dark speck of the Orphanage's roof glinted on the hills above Belle-on-Sea.

Bridget adjusted the utility belt—from which hung boxes and blobs and foil-wrapped lumps—and tied her hair in a ponytail.

"You don't need to come with me," she told Pascal.

The elf looked shocked.

"You don't think I can handle myself in sugary combat?" he said.

"No, I just mean—"

"You think I'm afraid?"

"Well, yes, and so am I, it's just that—"

"We Butters are never found wanting when the chips are down,"

said Pascal, with a firm nod. "We *love* chips."

"Great," said Bridget, wheeling the rickety old bicycle from the alley beside the shop. "You want to go in the basket?"

Pascal scrambled up the wheel.

"Lead on, my lady!" he said, thrusting a fist toward the sky.

Bridget lifted her leg over the bar and balanced awkwardly on her tiptoes.

Pascal, still posing heroically, raised his eyebrows.

"Lead on?" he said.

"I've never ridden a bike before," said Bridget. "I'm trying to figure it out."

"Never?" said Pascal.

"No! It's not like Miss Acrid would give us lessons, is it? She'd just have been adding another means of escape. But they say you never forget how to ride a bike, don't they?"

"Ye-es, but—"

"Well, then. I'll pretend I've done it before, then remember how."

She hopped onto the saddle, which creaked. The bike was much too tall, and they teetered for a few precarious moments.

"Bridget?" said Pascal.

Bridget looked at the chain, and the handlebars, and closed her eyes to find her center of balance.

"Don't worry," she said, locking her feet on the pedals, "I've got it!"

The bike leaped forward, pedals flying with a rusty squeak as they raced toward the Orphanage.

Pascal dropped into the basket and gripped its edge, his eager face peeking out at the road ahead.

"You're a marvel!" he cried, grinning madly. "You're a wonder!"

"We're coming for you, Mr. V!" Bridget called as they sped down Candlewick Place onto the winding country road. "We're coming!"

Suction Cupcakes 3

Bridget rose from the saddle as they rattled over the cobbles in the Orphanage's sweeping driveway, then hopped silently to the ground.

Pascal leaped from the basket, rolling as he hit the dirt. The bike careered into a bush, then fell over.

"Right," said Bridget, scuttling behind a hedge before patting her belt and straps. "We've got everything we need. Are you ready?"

"You bet your sweet little crumpet I'm ready!" he growled, thumping his chest.

"You're very hyped up," said Bridget, stroking his head.

"You're cheese flan right I am!" screamed Pascal.

"What's the plan?"

Bridget checked over a heavy, metal box strapped to her waist, then folded her hands.

"The plan is a careful infiltration of the Orphanage for Errant Childs, using baked goods as tools and weapons where practical to complete our mission. Patience is key—we can't just burst in the door and start throwing Razor Buns. Miss Acrid seems like a big nincompoop, but she's crafty. And after years of me trying to escape, playing pranks and making her look silly, she knows the full range of my invention and trickery."

"Oh," said Pascal, sagging slightly.

"But she won't see this coming," Bridget added.

"How do you know?"

Bridget grinned.

"Because she's never seen me bake before."

She reached into a pocket of her utility belt and rubbed stripes of dark chocolate across her face.

When she opened her eyes, they were bright and clear.

"Oh, my," said Pascal. "A confectionary commando."

Bridget smudged his face as well.

The girl and the elf regarded each other solemnly.

"We know something nobody else knows, Pascal. Nobody in the world."

"Do we?"

"Yes. Everyone thinks that baking is for making things you can *eat*. But we know different."

Pascal climbed onto her head and grabbed a couple of fistfuls of hair.

"No one's ever made jelly explode before," he said.

"Nope," said Bridget, stepping out from the shadow of the hedge.

"No one's ever cut wood with a bun before."

"Never."

"No one's ever made super-sticky cupcakes or screaming cream before."

"And that makes me," said Bridget, looking up the cliff face of the gigantic wall, "the best there is."

She unclipped four foil-wrapped lumps from her shoulder straps, fastened one to each foot, then gripped one in each hand.

"Time to see how sticky these Suction Cupcakes really are, wouldn't you say?"

"Absolutely," said Pascal.

Bridget puffed out her cheeks.

She raised her foot, as though climbing an invisible ladder, so that their combined weight was held by a single smear of vanilla frosting.

They looked up.

Miss Acrid's office window was blazing with light—hundreds of feet in the air.

"Is this going to work?" asked Pascal.

"Absolutely," said Bridget. Then, because she never lied, she added, "Probably."

"Probably?"

Bridget nodded.

"We've never tested how *long* the icing stays sticky. And it's *cold*—we need to hope it doesn't freeze."

Pascal gave Bridget a kiss on the top of her head.

"I trust you," he said.

Bridget thinned her lips—and began to climb.

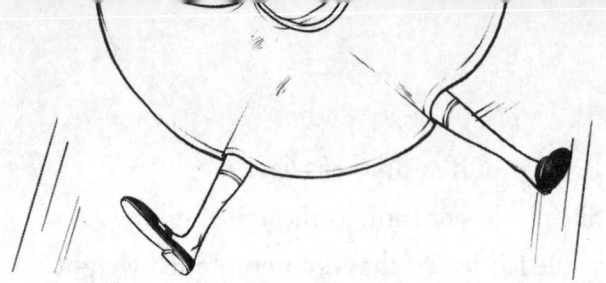

33

Jump

paraskirt ✳ icy winds ✳ falling upward

Dark, billowing clouds had formed over the sea, blown by a winter wind that smashed against the Orphanage wall and blew Bridget's skirt and hair up in a freezing frenzy, threatening to pull her from her three-hundred-foot-high perch.

"Keep going, Bridget," Pascal shouted over the roar of the wind. "You're doing brilliantly!"

"How . . . much . . . farther . . . ?" Bridget managed through her teeth, stretching to thud a cupcake over her head and pulling, heaving, straining to lift her chest up to its height.

The wind whipped at them again. Bridget's ears

felt sore, and her eyes and nose were beginning to stream.

She hugged the wall. The cupcake cases were beginning to frost over, and she flexed her fingers to keep away the chill.

"You're nearly halfway," said Pascal.

"*Halfway?*" said Bridget. "Oh, Pascal! If this was July, when it's nice and warm with no wind ... but I can't feel my hands! We're not going to make it!"

"Come on, Bridget, I believe in you! You can do it!"

Bridget's fingers began to slip from the cupcakes' icy paper.

She glanced down. The cobblestones, so far distant, looked like fish scales.

"It's too *cold*," she said. "My hands are slipping! And one of my ... feet ... is ... stuck!"

She heaved with all her might—but the Suction Cupcake was stuck fast, the icing frozen solid to the stone.

Come on, Bridget, said Tom's voice in her head. *You always win.*

"Yes," Bridget said aloud. "I do."

She shook her head and gritted her teeth,

running frantically through her mental map of the Orphanage's tunnels, exits and corridors.

"If we're halfway," she yelled above the roar of the wind, "there should be a mop cupboard with a porthole, a little above us, in the direction of the sea. Can you see it?"

Pascal looked up. A white ribbon of moonlight bounced from a round window above them.

"Yes, it's there!" He clapped. "Can you climb sideways with only three Suction Cupcakes?"

"Try *two* cupcakes!" shouted Bridget, as the cupcake in her left hand fused to the frost-covered wall.

"Oh, no!" wailed Pascal. "What are we going to do? We're going to fall!"

Bridget thought quickly.

"No," she said, crouching against the wall. "We're going to jump!"

"*WHAT?*" screamed Pascal. "Bridget, no, I don't think—"

"Ready..." Bridget shouted.

"No! I'm not! I can't—"

"Steady..."

"*Aaaaaaaaaaargh!*" wailed Pascal, grabbing as

much of Bridget's hair as he could and closing his eyes.

"Go!"

Bridget leaped from the wall like a frog, turning a somersault so that for a moment she hung in midair, hundreds of feet above the ground.

She closed her eyes.

The wind hit them from below like a train, opening her paraskirt and *lifting* them upward, up, up, up so that, as she spread her arms and grinned, Bridget *flew* toward the mop cupboard with the porthole window.

"Good heavens!" cried Pascal. "You can *fly*?"

Bridget tensed as they got closer, spinning gently in the air so they landed with a bump right in the center of the windowsill.

"More like falling upward," she said, backing them into the shelter of the window frame.

They glanced down.

The Suction Cupcakes stuck out from the wall like blisters, already white with the growing frost.

"That was lucky," said Pascal.

"I always find that the more ingenious I am," said Bridget, smoothing her paraskirt, "the luckier I get."

Pascal climbed onto Bridget's shoulder and they leaned against the window. Bridget felt the elf's little heart thrumming, like a pulled string, against her palm.

"You're freezing," she said, reaching into her utility belt. "Let's get inside."

Razor Buns 3

"Are you sure this is going to work?" said Pascal. The wind had picked up again, and his moustache was whirling around his face.

"Definitely," said Bridget. "Diamond cuts glass, after all — and the only thing sharper than diamond is one of my Razor Buns."

She pulled on leather gloves then, as carefully as she could, took a Razor Bun from the box on her shoulder strap and brushed its edge against the stone wall.

A sliver of stone, fine as a beetle's wing, peeled away.

"Your baking really is quite something," gulped Pascal.

"Best worst baker in the world," said Bridget.

She pressed the Razor Bun to the windowpane. A bloom of white cracks shot out around it.

"Amazing," said Pascal, his teeth rattling as he spoke.

Bridget moved the bun's edge around the perimeter of the window, tracing a line with a needling noise that poked through their ears to the inside of their skulls.

"I'm not sure I can take much more of that!" shouted Pascal, hands clamped over his head.

Bridget chuckled.

"Won't be long. What delicate little ears you have." She stopped in alarm. "Just like Miss Acrid."

She pictured the noise of slicing glass shooting through the Orphanage corridors in arrows of piercing sound, before ending up, as everything did—every secret, rumor and hint of mischief—in Miss Acrid's twitching earholes.

"We need to hurry!" she cried. "She'll have heard us!"

Pascal pressed his face to the glass.

"Miss Acrid's not in there yet—just a bunch of buckets and brushes!"

Bridget swirled the Razor Bun around the top of the window. Her hair was being tugged by the wind, and freezing bursts of air rushed up the wall, filling the paraskirt and threatening to drag her from the windowsill and send her floating helplessly back to earth.

She had *nearly* cut out a perfect, full circle of glass.

"There's a shadow under the door!" screamed Pascal. "Look!"

Bridget saw the dark, unmistakable shape.

"Leave her to me," she said, reaching into her utility belt.

She cut through the last of the glass, pushed the pane into the room and, clutching Pascal to her chest, leaped into the mop cupboard.

They landed with a clatter of buckets and scattering brooms.

Miss Acrid's shadow froze.

"Is that *you*, Baxter?" she hissed. "Glad to be *home*, are we?"

Bridget scowled.

"My home is in Vanderpuff's Bake Shop," she said. "And I've come to collect my guardian."

"You're too late!" shrieked the Mistress. "Vandalwharf is locked up in the dungeon, trapped behind some brand-new, *unpickable* locks! And now you've got yourself locked in the mop cupboard, boo-hoo—I guess you'll have to stay there forever and ever!"

Bridget spun the frost-covered Razor Bun and caught it—*very* carefully—in midair.

"I don't think so," she said, slicing through the solid, wooden door with a single swipe of the bun.

The door fell apart in great chunks of wood, revealing a corridor beyond teeming with booby traps: a spider's web of trip wires, dangling blades and deadly spikes.

"Hello, Stinky," said Bridget, reaching into a pouch on her utility belt. "Remember me?"

Miss Acrid took a step forward. Bridget could smell the fish on her breath.

"My door!" she cried. "Oh, you'll pay for that, gal, you'll—what's that?"

Bridget looked at the small tin she was holding.

"This?" she said innocently. "It's just a little cream."

And she dropped the tin.

Scream Cream 3

The Scream Cream landed with a splat.

Miss Acrid glanced at it, then took a menacing clomp toward Bridget.

"So, what, I'm supposed to *slip* on it or something? Don't you know I've got the surest foots there are, gal?"

Bridget pressed some dough into her ears, then handed the rest to Pascal.

"What are you doing?" demanded Miss Acrid.

"Ssh," said Bridget.

And the Scream Cream *screamed*.

Miss Acrid fell to her knees, fists gripping her ears.

"My ears!" she cried. "My delicate lugs!"

Bridget darted round her, leaping over a flailing boot.

"What now?" yelled Pascal, straining to be heard over the cream's deafening roar.

The corridor of booby traps stretched out ahead of them.

"We get Mr. Vanderpuff back," shouted Bridget.

Miss Acrid began to rise, her face livid with angry veins.

"Then let's go!" cried the elf, hopping anxiously. "She's coming!"

Bridget looked at the blades swinging from the ceiling.

"Wait," she said.

Miss Acrid was now fully upright, her furious gaze fixed on them.

"We can't *wait*!" cried Pascal. "She's coming!"

"Wait!" said Bridget, eyes on the ceiling.

The Scream Cream was running around wildly.

Its cries were shaking the Orphanage's very walls, and the blades were teetering like autumn leaves.

Ready to fall.

"Let's go!" shouted Pascal.

"If we go, those blades will cut us in two!" said Bridget. "We need to let them," the first blade juddered into the ground like a stuck arrow, "drop."

Miss Acrid lunged, grabbing the Scream Cream in a wriggling, liquid blob.

"Aha!" she cried, triumphant. "I've got you now, you wailing dairy!"

And she threw the cream out the window.

The screams faded slowly, taken by the wind.

Miss Acrid, splodgy with spilled cream, turned to Bridget with a nasty leer.

The rest of the dangling blades shattered on the ground.

"How *dare* you make such a mess!" howled the Mistress. "Oh, you always were a little *wretch*! And you can bet I'm going to lock that dungeon up good once I get you inside! There'll be no escaping *this* time, not on your nelly!"

She shot forward, her grabbing mitts missing Bridget's hair by inches.

Bridget hopped onto a windowsill and thudded two Suction Cupcakes at Miss Acrid's feet.

The great boots landed on the icing.

"What now?" screamed Miss Acrid, heaving against the cupcakes' grip. "You little *witch*! I'm going to . . . when I . . ."

"Stick around," said Bridget, hefting a Razor Bun in each hand. She spun the lethal buns through the air. The trip wires snapped with a *twang* as the buns cut them asunder, the whole web of cables splitting apart in the onslaught of sharpened flour.

"No!" howled Miss Acrid, straining once more for Bridget's neck.

"Come on," Bridget

whispered, nodding to Pascal.

And she ran, darting between the porcupine of spikes, toward Miss Acrid's distant office.

"Come *back* this instant!" shouted the Mistress, frantically unlacing her boots and plonking her bare, cheesy feet on the floor.

Bridget kept going, past empty dormitories with their curtains flapping like ghosts, past the library full of wonderful books, past the kitchen and the canteen and the bathroom with its leaking taps. The smells of the place—the disinfectant, the rubber-soled shoes, the overwhelming chill of cold, damp stone—filled her gasping lungs as she sped up the stairs toward the Mistress's office and the entrance to the dungeon.

"She's coming!" shouted Pascal.

"Mr. V is behind that door," she said, as Miss Acrid's barefoot stomp echoed around them. "Let's go and get him."

36

Rescue

love ✻ Pascal appears ✻ Rescue

"No!" screamed Miss Acrid, bursting through the door after them. Her beehive hairstyle had wilted, like a soggy weed, over one eye.

Bridget tossed Pascal onto a high shelf and rolled clear of the Mistress's stamping feet.

The trapdoor, she saw, was locked and bolted—and heavy iron bars had been laid across it.

"Vandypump is one of my Errant Childs now!" Miss Acrid went on. "He was errant enough to want *you* for a daughter, errant enough to *kidnap* you, and errant enough to come looking for some silly trinket your *friend* gave you. He *belongs* to me! You *both* belong to me! And you shall stay here *forever!*"

Bridget fumbled with her utility belt—but Miss Acrid was too quick, and ripped it away.

"You've got no tricks now, gal!" she yelled, stamping toward Bridget. "What are you without your little *tools* and *inventions*? You're *nothing*, that's what! *Nothing!*"

"That's not true," said Bridget quietly.

"Stop mumbling, gal!" screamed Miss Acrid, swiping at her again.

"That's not true!" shouted Bridget, rising to her full height. "I'm a kind person, and I'm a good friend. I'm *loved*, and that's something you'll never understand!"

"*Loved!*" snarled Miss Acrid, grabbing Bridget by the collar and holding her aloft. "Who could ever love a child who spoils and shatters and *ruins* everything she touches? A naughty, noisy, *dreamy* child?"

Bridget sagged in her grip.

"Who," Miss Acrid said, leaning in until her breath filled Bridget's mouth, "could ever love *you*?"

"I do!" yelled Pascal.

And he leaped from his high shelf onto Miss Acrid's astonished face.

"What is that?" said the Mistress, slapping at her cheeks to shift the furious elf. "It's an invisible monster! Get it away!"

"I'm *not* invisible!" shouted Pascal, lifting one of Miss Acrid's eyelids in each hand. "The people I love can see me! Etta Vanderpuff could see me! Bridget Baxter can see me! And you, fish face, can definitely *feel* this!"

He let go of Miss Acrid's eyelids, which snapped back in place with a smack.

"Gah!" cried the Mistress, stumbling backward.

Bridget hit the ground and rolled.

She watched Pascal fighting for her, and felt the fire roar in her heart.

"This ends here, Acrid!" she shouted. "No more Errant Childs, no more Orphanage!"

Miss Acrid lunged for Pascal—but the elf was already back on his shelf, and she fell to her knees.

Bridget clenched her fists. "I've got some treats for you," she said, popping more dough into her ears. "Open wide."

"*Gah!*" screamed Miss Acrid.

She grabbed her salmon-sword from above the fireplace and rushed forward, swinging wildly.

Bridget stepped nimbly to the side, watching in slow motion as the blade whipped past, millimeters from her nose—and at that exact moment, she splashed it with another tin of Scream Cream.

"*Oh . . . ohhhhh, nooooo!*" yelled Miss Acrid as the cream screamed louder and louder, shaking the sword like a ruler twanged on the edge of a desk.

Holding on to the sword for dear life, Miss Acrid was shaken into a wailing blur.

"*Aaaaaaarrrrrrrrrrrggggggggghhhhhhhhhhhh!*" she screamed, as she buzzed round the floor.

Bridget dived for cover—and stuck out a leg.

Miss Acrid fell, face first, and threw the sword through the window.

It dropped to the ground, screaming all the way. Cold wind whipped into the office, whirling their hair around their faces.

Miss Acrid dragged her soggy fringe back onto her forehead. One of her eyes was twitching.

"You're going to *regret* that," she growled.

Bridget bowed her head, then looked up through her curtain of hair.

"You still don't remember, do you, Miss?" she said, unclipping two more Suction Cupcakes from her straps. "You only regret the things you *don't* do."

And she threw the cupcakes at Miss Acrid's face. They landed on her eyebrows with a soggy *thurrrp*.

"Yes!" said Pascal, punching the air. "That'll teach her!"

"My brows!" screamed Miss Acrid, grabbing at the cupcakes.

"I wouldn't do that if I was you," said Bridget, hopping into the Mistress's chair and putting her feet on the desk.

"You cheeky little . . . How *dare* you place your horrid little bot in my leather throne! I'm going to wring your . . . as soon as I . . ."

Miss Acrid heaved at the cupcakes as hard as she could. Then she tried to pull her hands free.

"A particularly sticky batch," said Bridget. "Exactly what I was hoping for."

"Curse you, horrid rat!"

Miss Acrid heaved once more at her stuck hands, pulling until her neck grew red and her shoulders began to tremble, and then, with a slow, tearing, sucking sound, the Suction Cupcakes came free.

Taking every single hair of the Mistress's precious monobrow with them.

"My *brow*!" she screamed, her eyes wide with horror. "You've done it this time!"

She rushed forward, swinging her Suction Cupcake hands—but

as she went to grab Bridget in a crushing bear hug, Bridget ducked and slid between her feet, leaving the Mistress hugging herself as tightly as she could, her hands stuck to her own shoulders.

She stumbled against the shelves of hideous things.

The dodo dropped onto her head.

A marble bust fell on her foot.

A flutter of unread books landed on her wilted beehive.

And the biggest jar shattered on her head.

Eyeballs rolled everywhere as the Mistress slumped to the ground, her own eyes rolling dizzily. She was wrapped securely in a sticky vanilla straitjacket, and she winced as Bridget stood over her.

"What are you going to do?" she snarled.

Bridget reached for her utility belt.

"Do your worst!" shouted Miss Acrid.

"I'm not afraid of you!"

Bridget smirked, and unclipped a croissant.

"What does that do?" asked Miss Acrid. "What is it? A rocket? A bomb? Are you going to electrocute me? What?"

"Just you wait," said Bridget, tearing a piece of croissant and moving it toward Miss Acrid's mouth.

"*Aaaaaaaargh!*" screamed the Mistress.

"Baking is best when it's shared, you know," said Bridget.

And she pushed the croissant into Miss Acrid's mouth.

Miss Acrid's face contorted in disgust.

"That is horrible!" she spluttered. "Good grief! This is even *worse* than the noisy cream or the sticky cakes or the sharp buns! You can't *eat* any of this stuffs! You're a *bad* baker, Baxter—a bad *bad* baker!"

"No, Miss," Bridget said happily. "I'm the *worst* baker in the whole world."

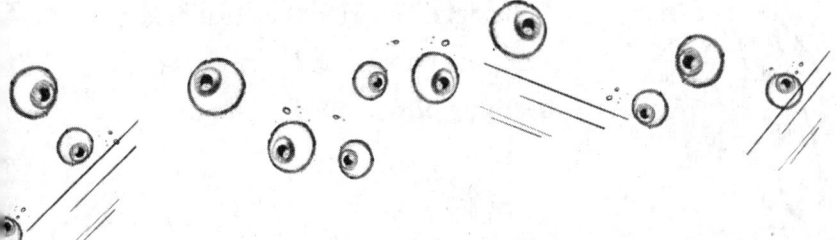

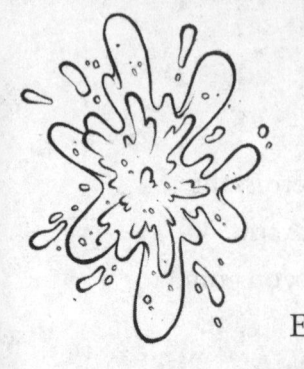

Carefully, delicately, she poured Jellymite on the trapdoor's heavy bolts, then stood back.

"You once told me I was the last Errant Child," she said. "Do you remember that? You wanted me to be lonely and sad. You *laughed* about it."

Miss Acrid grinned.

"It was funny," she said.

Pascal gasped.

"Well," said Bridget, smiling at her tin of Jellymite, "I'm going to make *sure* I'm the last Errant Child—*ever*."

The Jellymite exploded with a mighty *BOOM*, throwing the trapdoor up like a tiddlywink.

Bridget grabbed Pascal and, together, they slid down the helter-skelter into the dungeon—into Mr. Vanderpuff's waiting arms.

She struck him right in the middle of the chest, and they landed in a giddy, chuckling heap.

"Bridget!" cheered the great baker, propping himself on his elbows and beaming down at her. "Oh, my dear, I knew you'd come for me!"

"Of course!" said Bridget, giving him a big squeeze.

Mr. Vanderpuff stroked her hair, and sighed deeply.

"We both came for you," said Pascal, dusting himself down. "It's the least a Butters could do for his captain."

Mr. Vanderpuff blinked rapidly. Then he took off his glasses, cleaned them, put them back on, and blinked again.

"You're my elf," he said, looking Pascal in the face. "Aren't you?"

Pascal beamed.

"Pascal La Fleur at your *service*, sah!" he said, saluting with happy tears on his cheeks.

Mr. Vanderpuff returned his salute.

"I *remember* now!" he said, shaking Pascal's hand. "Etta used to sing to you, while I was in my inventing room . . . and you'd help me with the little jobs in the bakery. Where have you been?"

Pascal threw his arms around Mr. Vanderpuff's neck.

"I got a bit lost for a while," he said, his moustache

trembling. "But I'm back now."

"Are you all right, Mr. V?" asked Bridget. "Did Miss Acrid hurt you?"

There was a thump overhead.

"Not at all," said Mr. Vanderpuff. "She put me to work making her cakes—she was planning to kidnap a whole bunch of cooks and chefs so she could keep the most delicious food for herself. But not anymore! You saved me!"

Bridget blew the dust off a Razor Bun, and grinned.

"It was nothing," she said. "Let's go home."

Tom

Reunion ✶ Wintersmith Fete ✶ a new name

"Careful... careful..." said Mr. Vanderpuff.

Bridget met his eyes as they lowered the last layer of the Wintersmith Cake into place.

They had made it, together, in the newly re-opened inventing room, right under the smiling face of Etta Vanderpuff, her portrait beaming down on the mixing table.

"What is it?" asked Mr. Vanderpuff.

Bridget grinned.

"Just that I've never managed to finish a cake before without there being, you know... fires

and screaming."[37]

Mr. Vanderpuff chuckled.

"I think we're a perfect team, don't you? This is going to be the most amazing cake anyone has ever seen!"

Bridget squeezed Tom's ring. She hadn't taken it off since Mr. Vanderpuff had retrieved it from Miss Acrid's office, and its happy energy was pulsing through her like the chords of a beautiful song.

She looked around. The fete glowed with the warmth of candles and laughter, its mulled-wine lagoon breathing cinnamon smoke into the crisp, starry sky. Mrs. Pobydd and Mr. Falstaff strolled happily arm in arm, while children ran between the stalls, their cheeks red from laughter and play. The air was filled with delicious smells: sausages and chestnuts and rosemary and candy floss.

"It's snowing," said Pascal.

"So it is," said Mr. Vanderpuff. He tilted his head. "I really am glad to have you back, my little elf. I feel more . . . myself, now that you're here.

---

[37] There had been one *very* small fire, on the tip of Pascal's moustache, which *had* made him scream a bit—but the elf had taken full responsibility, so Bridget was off the hook.

Does that make sense?"

Pascal twiddled his moustache shyly.

"Total sense, sir," he said.

Bridget turned to Mr. Vanderpuff.

"You really think this'll be the best cake ever?" she asked.

"Of *course*! How could it not be! Three layers of wonderfully flavored sponges: caramel, chocolate and lemon; with sumptuous jellies and jams from my jam cupboard. And with *your* ingenious contributions, it'll be the talk of the town! The country! The world!"

"Good evening, Mr. Vanderpuff," said the mayor, arriving at the front of the bake shop. She was carrying a cup of steaming, clove-smelling wine. She looked very cozy, and very pleased. "And good evening, Miss Baxter. Thank you for passing on your concerns about the Orphanage for Errant Childs. Miss Acrid is now in the hands of the police, and the building itself, well . . . it's odd. *Impossible*, even."

"What is, ma'am?" asked Mr. Vanderpuff.

"It's been destroyed! Crumbled to dust, not a stone left standing—apart from the *library*."

"The library?"

"Yes. It's the strangest thing—the library is perfectly intact. It's sitting there, not a page out of place, in the middle of this frightful ruin!"

"Amazing," said Mr. Vanderpuff.

"What are you going to do with it?" asked Bridget.

"I'm going to open it up to the village, of course! Those beautiful books deserve to be *read*, don't you think?"

"I really do!" said Bridget. "Is that *all* you found up there?"

The mayor clicked her teeth.

"Now you come to mention it," she said, "there was a *smell* . . ."

"Smell, ma'am?"

"Yes," said the mayor. "Sort of cold, and . . . citrusy. Almost like, well," she chuckled, "like *jelly*."

"How strange," said Mr. Vanderpuff.

Bridget squeezed his hand.

"I know!" said the mayor, shrugging. "Now, I'm just about to declare the Wintersmith Fete officially open! Is everything ready? Your cake will be the star attraction, as ever. What can you tell me about it?"

"Bridget?" said Mr. Vanderpuff, with a wink.

Bridget took a deep breath.

"Three tiers of genoise sponge, filled with different flavors of Vanderpuff's jam, and . . . my own inventions . . ."

"*Your* inventions?" said the mayor, with a delighted clap. "How wonderful! Tell me, what are they?"

"Well," said Bridget, pointing at the decorations, "the cake has a Razor Bun finish, Musical Scream Cream piping, a Jellymite glaze and a Suction Cupcake base."

The mayor frowned.

"And what does that mean?" she asked.

"It means," said Bridget, "that the cake cuts itself with the Razor Buns, while the Musical Scream Cream sings a lovely song, followed by a miniature Jellymite firework display."

The mayor clapped in delight.

"And the Suction Cupcakes?"

Bridget smiled.

"Your slice never slides off the plate."

"Isn't it *wonderful*!" cried Mr. Vanderpuff, gripping Bridget's shoulders. "She's a *genius* in the bakery, Madam Mayor, she really is. *Musical* cream? Miniature, edible fireworks? I could *never* have dreamed up such things on my own! Of course, you shall have the first slice!"

The mayor nodded graciously.

"I think we'll be seeing rather a lot of each other, Miss Baxter," she said. "Belle-on-Sea is very glad to have you."

"Thank you, ma'am," said Bridget.

"Boy, was the mayor impressed with you, Bridget," said Pascal. "You're going to be a hero in this town, you wait!"

"Oh," said Bridget. "I don't want to be a hero. I just want to stay here."

"And so you shall," said Mr. Vanderpuff.

Together, they stacked the plates on the little table. Bridget busied herself folding the napkins, imagining the looks on people's faces when they heard their cake singing to them for the first time.[38]

"I knew you'd save me," said Mr. Vanderpuff. "When I was in that dungeon, I wasn't worried for a second, because I knew you'd be coming to get me."

"How?" said Bridget. "How did you know for sure?"

"Because I love you very much," said Mr. Vanderpuff. "And I know you're capable of amazing things."

Bridget sighed happily.

"I love you, too," she said.

"Well," said Mr. Vanderpuff. "Isn't that lovely? Now, we've got some important people to say hello to—the town's new dentists. Dentists are

---

[38] Depending on which slice you received, you would hear a different song—anything from "Look Out, Mr. Chipmunk!" to "It Wasn't My Weasel's Woggle." Bridget was working on a cake that took requests.

sometimes a bit wary of me, what with all the sugar and everything, but this couple wants to come and meet us."

"They do?" said Bridget.

"Yes. Meet *you*, as a matter of fact."

"*Me?* Are you sure? I don't—" Bridget froze.

A familiar voice rang out from the crowd.

She turned to look, hardly daring to breathe.

Tom was walking along Candlewick Place between a well-dressed couple who occasionally fussed with his hair or touched his cheek.

And his smile was fixed on Bridget.

"It's Tom," whispered Bridget.

Mr. Vanderpuff followed her gaze.

"Why don't you go and say hello, my dear?" he said, smiling broadly. "I can finish setting up here."

Bridget hugged the great baker's waist, and they held each other as the snow fell.

Pascal tucked himself under her arm. Mr. Vanderpuff kissed the top of her head.

"I once told you that everyone needs rescuing," he said. "But I thought I was rescuing *you*."

"What do you mean?" asked Bridget.

Mr. Vanderpuff crouched before her and wiped

away her happy tears.

"It was *you* who rescued *me*, Bridget Baxter."

Bridget threw her arms around his neck.

"What do you think of 'Bridget Vanderpuff'?" she said.

"Oh," gasped Mr. Vanderpuff, his hand in Bridget's hair. "I think it's rather wonderful."

"Me too, Dad," said Bridget, squeezing him as tightly as she could. "Me too."

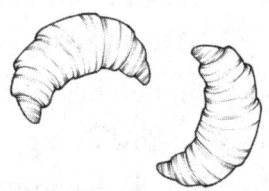

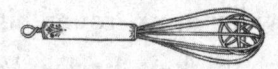

Acknowledgments

The transition from drafting alone to editorial teamwork is always lovely, and I've been very lucky that Bridget has found such a wonderful home with the good people of Zephyr.

To my editor, Lauren Atherton, for her guidance, insight, and passion for this series; to Fiona Kennedy, for her support from the beginning; to Megan Pickford, for nailing the title; and to Anne-Marie Hansen for taking Bridget abroad! To Hannah Featherstone for catching my inaccuracies, and to Sabina Maharjan and Courtney Jefferies of EDPR for their work promoting the world of Belle-on-Sea.

To David Habben, for bringing Bridget's world so vividly to life; to my agent, Molly Ker Hawn, for somehow making this happen, again; and to Tom Bonnick, whose interest in Bridget's original incarnation meant that this one got finished. To my friends (Peter Crouch?) and family for their continuous support, and to Harte of Troon, for baking real-life Vanderpuff treats! To Jim Baird for possessing not expertise but the contact details of experts; and to Gary Maclean, for his generosity of both time and knowledge.

Thank you.

To my children, Tessie and Milo, who bake with me now; to my mum and my gran, who baked with me then; and to my wife, Julie, whose love is the inspiration for the magical home Bridget finds. Thank you, for everything. I love you all.

Pascal's Bake Generator

Raspy	berry	Pop
Cara	tastic	Tart
Coffee	wonder	Swirl
Sweetie	tasty	Trifle

Name Your Bake Here!

Hello, Bakers!

Welcome to Pascal's Patented Vanderpuff Bake Generator, where you can design your very own Vanderpuff bake!

Simply pick one word from each column, then put them together. You might create a Raspy-tastic Swirl, or a Cara-wonder Tart, a Coffee-berry Pop, or a Sweetie-tasty Trifle. You could even make up your own brand-new words!

And don't stop there—bring it to life! Oh, draw it, make it with clay—even bake it! You could ask a grown-up to help upload a picture to Instagram using the hashtag *#BridgetBakes*.

I can't wait to see your creations!

> Love and lemons!
> *Pascal La Fleur*

Choco Chipoconut Recipe

Choco Chipoconuts were on the shelves the day I opened my bake shop, and they're still there now! These delightful little cookies are squidgy, gooey, crunchy, fudgy, and quite scrumdiddlyicious. I like mine with a glass of cold milk—you, of course, may enjoy yours however you wish!

*I find they go best with warm pajamas
and a good book!
— Pascal*

*The oats and coconut create a wonderful chewiness that makes it very difficult to have just one Choco Chipoconut
(we sell them by the baker's dozen).
I hope you have fun making them!
— Ernest Vanderpuff*

Recipe on next page ➡

Choco Chipoconut Recipe

About the chef

Gary Maclean is Scotland's national chef, and a former winner of *Masterchef: The Professionals*. He believes passionately that children should be involved in their food's journey, from shop to cupboard to plate, and that principle—the importance of spending time together, talking about ingredients and making wonderful things—is manifest in Mr. Vanderpuff's commitment to Bridget's baking lessons!

The following recipe can be found in Gary's excellent book, *Kitchen Essentials*. For more information about Gary and his work, visit garymacchef.com.

Ingredients

Pinch of salt

1 cup self-rising flour

½ cup shredded coconut

½ cup quick oats

¼ cup butter

¾ cup dark brown sugar

1 egg, beaten

½ tsp vanilla extract

½ cup semisweet chocolate chips

Parchment paper to line your baking tray

Method

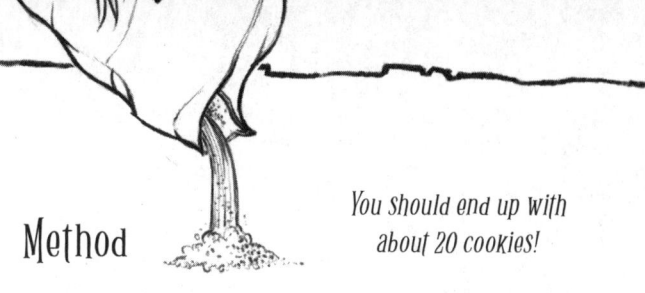

You should end up with about 20 cookies!

1. First, politely ask your elf to preheat the oven to 325°F.
2. Mix the salt, flour, coconut, and oats together in a bowl.
3. Now cream the butter and sugar together until it's light and fluffy. *I find it's much easier (and more fun!) to do this with your hands.*
4. Add the beaten egg and vanilla extract, then the chocolate chips!
5. Add the buttery, sugary, eggy, vanilla, chocolate chip mixture to the bowl of flour—then combine into a lovely dough.
6. Roll the dough until it's around 1/4-inch thick (*or as thick as an elf's thumbnail!*).
7. Cut out the Choco Chipoconuts. A round 3-inch cookie cutter works best.
8. Bake in the oven on a tray lined with parchment paper for 10 minutes.
9. Allow them to cool on a wire rack.
10. Share your Choco Chipoconuts with someone you love!

Martin Stewart
is a former English teacher
who lives on the west coast of
Scotland with his wife, two
children, and a very big dog.

David Habben
is an artist, illustrator,
and educator living
in Utah, USA.

Help Bridget solve the mystery in her next adventure!

It is the Night of the Hungry Ghosts. A ghost train is seen rattling into town. People have gone missing. Someone—or some*thing*—is out to destroy Belle-on-Sea. And sabotage Mr. V's bake for the Hungry Ghosts parade. With her best friend, Tom, Bridget uses her incredible powers of invention and detection to solve the mystery in her second spooky adventure. Happy Hallowe'en!

Bridget Vanderpuff is a super-sleuthing, mystery-solving inventor.

She is the Best Worst Baker in the World!

www.bridgetvanderpuff.com